E. Eltinge Hosier

Gnitle, the Sunbeam

E. Eltinge Hosier

Gnitle, the Sunbeam

ISBN/EAN: 9783744746359

Printed in Europe, USA, Canada, Australia, Japan

Cover: Foto ©Andreas Hilbeck / pixelio.de

More available books at **www.hansebooks.com**

BY

E. ELTINGE HOSIER.

GOODMAN PRINTING & PUBLISHING CO.,
NEW YORK.
1890.

PREFACE.

One day in the Fall of 1876, while thinking of my heroine, I concluded to write a story that would not only be interesting, but ennobling to the young misses growing up around me. While glancing over books then published, I thought them too mature, otherwise not exactly suited for girls entering, or in their teens. When finished it was perfectly satisfactory to myself, but I preferred to have some one el· pa ;; judgment upon i·, so concluded to await the result. Having receive , a favorable report from the critics of Appleton, Scribner, and Collier, I concluded to place it before the public, that it may reach those for whom it is especially designed.

I have taken much pleasure and pains in its preparation. And if it accomplishes the purpose I anticipate, I shall be more than satisfied. Hoping and trusting such will be the result, I will now sign myself your very true friend, E. E. H

———o———

THESE PENNED REPORTS BY CRITICS WERE KINDLY PRESENTED TO THE AUTHOR.

This is a holiday child's book. It is written in a very homely, but appropriate style, and recounts the youthful experiences of Gnitle, an amiable young lady, full of fun and innocent mischief, to the time of her marriage. At first she assists her mother in teaching, and she is quite a model teacher. She lives with her mother and grandmother ; and their pleasant home makes a pretty picture in the story. Gnitle's first grief is when her mother thinks of marrying again, and this is told in a way to please children, especially girls. The marriage comes off at last, and Gnitle becomes more reconciled to the new state of things. There is not much of what would be called a plot, but the number of characters is considerable, and we have Christmas festivities, birthdays, and weddings, besides some grave occurrences, to occupy the attention of the juvenile reader. The tone throughout is wholesome and cheerful. The lessons of family affection, respect, and proper discipline, are taught by inference rather than by sermonizing, so that the book is not made dull by injudicious preaching. The book then is one to entertain little girls. It is not so well adapted to boys. It seems fairly to carry out the purpose of the writer. The success of the little work depends upon the present state of the market for juveniles.—*Appleton's*.

Plot and moral excellent, and well written. It is a story for misses in their teens, and older ones can read it with profit.—*Scribner's*.

My critic reports very favorably.—*Collier*.

CONTENTS.

CHAPTER I.

GNITLE was the youngest of three children. Her mother was a widow living in an old-fashioned house with her mother.

Gnitle soon became a great favorite of her grandma. I rather think she saw herself reflected occasionally, for the child looked as much like her as possible.

There were the same brown, expressive eyes, Roman nose, a finely chiseled mouth, forehead medium of a Grecian cast, dark brown hair, which was put in papers once or twice a week, as curls seemed necessary to complete and blend with her style of beauty.

Now, I have given you as short an introduction to my little favorite as possible, knowing little folks don't like to be kept in suspense. The only reason I write of her is to show how uncommon she was.

Gnitle's mother had received a State certificate which was a great honor; for not one in a hundred received one. The village school was taught by her and the eldest daughter. Of course, there must be no partiality shown to Gnitle, so this mischievous little minx was called out and sent back with a reprimand very often.

Gnitle's brother, who had always remained with his grandma and aunt on his father's side, was now brought home to dwell with them, in order to give him a thorough

English education. Being the only boy, he was indeed his mother's joy! And what happiness it gave her to find him studious and attentive.

At first he was a little wayward; but his mother's decision and his own good judgment soon overcame all that.

Evenings when other boys were playing and shouting outside, he was reading the history of some great general, perfectly oblivious to any noise outside or in. At the age of twelve his mother considered him a thorough English scholar, and asked him to choose some profession. He chose a mercantile life, and thus far it has been a successful one.

He was always fond of Gnitle; when she would tease him, instead of getting angry, he would act so manly and pleasant toward her, that she began to think him something more than ordinary. So a word or look from him was enough; and to this day she holds him in reverence.

As he is connected with it, I will tell you about a little sleigh ride:

"This ride was talked over for more than a week by the boys and girls at school. Each boy of course, had a sleigh, and every boy had a sister or cousin whom they were expected to take.

"Saturday came. We were to meet on a road where there was but little travel, so we were all there punctually at ten o'clock, with mittens, furs, and everything to make us comfortable. Soon the line was formed, and fifty little sleighs, drawn by fifty little rosy-cheeked boys, went gliding over the hard snow.

"Such a jolly time! Boys shouting 'You take my sister, and I'll take yours'! And then a little turn at snow-ball-ing, then on again over the bright snow. Just then they came to a bend in the road, and a loose horse came bounding past them. Gnitle and her brother were the last of this long line. The box on the sleigh that held Gnitle became loose, and over she went, box and all, in the snow. Her brother did not miss her immediately, they were going at such speed.

"On looking back to see what became of the horse, he beheld Gnitle trying to get out of the box. When she found the horse was far out of sight, her eyes began to sparkle, her cheeks wore a dimple as she thought how funny it would be to have them miss her. Soon her little laughing face was at the end of the line again, and all went merrily along, for it was almost twelve, the time each one was expecting a good dinner spread out for them at home.

"As soon as the little procession was seen coming up the hill, all the neighbors assembled at that end of the village to see them enter, exclaiming 'What a pretty sight, and how happy they all look'! They were indeed both happy and hungry.

"It was a day never to be forgotten. For some of that little party it is a bright oasis yet. So think Gnitle and her brother."

CHAPTER II.

AS yet I have shown you nothing uncommon in Gnitle's character. She was very lenient toward schoolmates. For instance, if she was approached by a little girl in this manner—"Don't you think so and so (mentioning the name) is very selfish"?

"I never found her so, if you have; perhaps she had given all away she could spare."

One time I said to her "Don't tell Fanny O—— any of your secrets."

"O, I don't have any," said she; "for if a thing is hard to keep myself, I surely don't wish to burden my schoolmates with it."

If a schoolmate told her any thing in confidence, it was to her a sealed book. She was very frank; if you displeased her, she would ask you for a reason and tell you her mind freely. The consequence was, the girls and boys all had a high opinion of Gnitle.

There was one little girl in the school she loved with her whole heart, and I can assure you she was one capable of loving a great deal.

The two were inseparable. If one was called out, the other was sure to follow; for Gnitle only had to catch Adel's eye to make her giggle, while Gnitle would be looking the picture of innocence. She would be sent quietly to her seat, and Adel would be called to occupy the old splint-bottomed chair. Hand in hand they walked to and from school, or roamed through the orchards in search of Johny-apples, bow-apples, and a great many other kinds. The orchard was owned by Adel's father, and was a great resort for children. There was a large leather factory near it, and that was owned by him too. A cousin of Gnitle's was general overseer, so they felt privileged to hop about the factory too.

One day they were greatly amused. Gnitle's cousin, a black eyed little fellow, put a little playmate in an empty vat, and every few minutes he would lift the cover and say "Nick, can you beeze"? Voice within would drawl out "Yes"! then down went the cover. This was repeated a number of times; but when his turn came to get in, away he scampered over the bridge toward home.

How many people, as well as children, like a joke at other's expense!

There were a great many hands employed in this factory; so Adel's father kept a store in order to supply these families with everything needful, even to wearing apparel. Beside he had a large store elsewhere, so he was obliged to be away from home very often.

Adel's mother died when Nenie was a baby, and a well-educated lady took charge of the children, six in number. The three eldest were boys and the other three girls.

Soon her father brought home a young wife from the city. She was pretty, and fond of riding horseback, and had little else to do, as she had her mother with her, and plenty of help.

"She is very strict," Del would say, "but very good."

The eldest daughter was sent away to a seminary. Adel and Nenie were instructed by Gnitle's mother. The boys had finished their education—the eldest and youngest attending the store. The other looking to the weighing of hides, bark, and other matters generally.

Every thing seemed to be in a flourishing condition, till one bright moonlight night, we were aroused from sleep to behold the factory all in flames. I never shall forget the bright moon looking down, and the flames rising as if in mockery. The next morning there were only a few loads of bark remaining, and fifty or more poor families without employment. Another was built with as little delay as possible, and the poorer hands were allowed to run an account at the store till work was furnished them.

The store was next door to Gnitle's, so many a good thing Adel and she received from the eldest son. They would fill their little pockets and sit in Adel's yard, under the big weeping willows, eating and laughing, and watch the little row boats go up and down the big pond, out in the channel, sometimes seated in the large swing fastened on the willows, which they would push back and forth with their little feet to the top of the hill, then away they swung far over the water.

This was great fun. When tired of this they would slip in the cellar kitchen and get in the good graces of the colored cook, Deaun. When she began to laugh, so Del could see her big white teeth, she felt her way was clear for making molasses candy.

Deaun was a good old soul, and did not forget that she had once been a little girl herself, so made it pleasant for them when she was not too busy. Poor old Deaun used to say "We are all born, but we are not buried," meaning we cannot tell what will befall us—a very true saying; but, my young readers, remember—

"Providence wisely has mingled the cup,
And the best council in all your distress
Is the stout watchword of 'Never give up.'"

CHAPTER III.

ONE day Gnitle's mother was visiting a friend, so Gnitle and her sister feeling somewhat lonesome, ran over to Del's. Her mother happened to be in the kitchen; Gnitle ran up to her as usual, expecting a kiss, but instead, she looked at her angrily, and said sternly "Gnitle, did you say the reason Laura is kept at boarding school is because I am so unkind to her"?

Gnitle, with a proud and injured look, said "I have said nothing of the kind; for I never knew it to say, so how could I say it"?

Her sister commenced to question her. Gnitle simply answered "I have given my word, isn't that enough"? Then without saying more, started home, forcing back the tears.

She of course told her dear grandma, who did not doubt her innocense, and felt very sorry to see her little pet so worried.

When her mother reached home, and heard what had happened, she went over to see Del's mother, and asked her of whom she received such information. She did not wish to tell, but finally said "Del told her."

Gnitle was more surprised and grieved than ever to think Del, whom she had always loved, would tell any little privacy they may have had between them, when it would be the means of separating them; but she said, finally, "I know I never said it. Now, mama, don't you believe me"?

"Yes, I do believe you told the truth; but Gnitle, I want you to pray to your heavenly Father, and ask Him to remind you if you have said it."

None of her family doubted her, still they were anxious to have the mystery cleared up.

The Summer days seemed long to poor Gnitle, for she missed her old playmate more than she was willing to admit, for her proud and sensitive nature had been deeply wounded.

Her grandma would often say "Gnitle, what are you thinking about"?

"Well, grandma, I was just trying to think whether I had ever said it."

"You are not worrying over that yet, I hope!" for she felt it was burdensome to Gnitle; and so it was a heavy burden for her—so sensitive.

Night after night she would lie awake, trying to refresh her memory. During one of these sleepless nights she composed a short poem. As she was not e years old, I will pen it:

"When ills beset our earthly course,
O then 'tis sweet to have recourse
To One we know will not withhold
One blessing, but them manifold
Will ever send to cheer our way,
Until we're called to join the lay
Of those who sing from day to day."

Fearing she would not remember, she arose cautiously so as not to awaken her mother; but when she had finished writing, and was folding the paper, her mother awoke and said "Why Gnitle, what are you doing up in the cold"?

She answered "I thought of something, and was just writing a little."

Her mother did not question her further, so she soon fell asleep. Again before daylight she awoke suddenly, and finding sleep impossible, sat up in bed, but tried not to disturb her mother till morning. But everything came so fresh to her mind, she felt too happy to wait.

Her mother was awake, and knew what her little daughter was thinking of, but kept quiet till Gnitle pushed her, and said "Mama, if I tell you something, will you promise not to mention it"?

"Yes, if it is a secret I should keep."

After hesitating a moment, she said "Mama, I think Del told me that one day when we were sitting on the old splint-bottomed chair. When she told me anything, and said 'now don't tell,' I always tried to forget it."

"Well," said her mother, smiling, "I think you succeeded pretty well"!

"Well, Gnitle added, "If she did tell me, she has thought I might speak of it, so it would reach her mother, and that she would be punished for saying so. I feel sorry for Del: for I believe she has suffered more than I have. I've kept it so long, and will never tell what I think till she confesses; so mama, don't say anything about it."

Her mother promised she would not, so there the matter rested.

It was now the last of Autumn, and they had not played together since early in the Spring; they had spoken to each other pleasantly, but nothing more. Gnitle pitied

Del, and spoke more kindly to her than ever when they chanced to meet, for she did not think Del meant to make trouble, but took this way of shielding herself. What a lenient nature! What a noble little creature to suffer so, and still bury it, and wait patiently to be exonerated! And all for what. Trying to keep or forget another's secret.

CHAPTER IV.

WINTER came ; Del and Gnitle were taken ill with inflamatory fever ; both were attended by the same physician, so they were able to hear from each other every day. That seemed to render great consolation to both. After weeks of sickness, Del began to improve slightly, while poor Gnitle remained delirious, and required the attention of her grandma and mother. The eldest daughter, meanwhile, took charge of the school, as she was capable to manage it. What a comfort that was to her widowed mother. When the little sufferer was herself again, she would say " O, mama, I am so tired. I have been flying, and my body was so heavy ! Don't let me sleep again ; try and keep me awake. Talk to me ; tell me about Del ; is she better " ?

" Yes, and wants to see you."

This pleased her. Smiling sweetly, she would fall asleep, but only to awake from a delirious state again, and say " I'm so tired " !

When these symptoms appeared, doctors then bled their patients. While the doctor opened the vein in Gnitle's arm, she was singing " Glory Hallelujah," words in a favorite hymn of her's.

When she came to herself, and found her arm bandaged, they told her why it was done, and what she had been singing the while, over which she laughed heartily.

Del was now able to walk out in the yard. One day she chanced to hear that Gnitle was not expected to live the night through, and then it was her conscience smote her. Consequently, she asked her nurse to wrap her up, and take her to the lower part of the garden. When they reached this part of it, she burst forth into tears, and said " Do you think Gnitle will die " ?

The nurse fearing to tell her, said " O, I believe the doctor still has hopes of her getting better."

"O, if I could only see her ! Go into the house and tell mother for me, Gnitle did not tell me that. It was I who told her one day when we were sitting on the old chair in the school room."

The nurse returned to the house without her, and told her mother all, and likewise how excited she seemed.

" Tell her I was greatly surprised, but only too glad to know the truth of the matter ; " but, she added, " I am so sorry that poor little Gnitle has been burdened with it so long. But Del is too weak to be excited, and she has suffered too much I fear already, so you may say I am pleased to know the truth, and that I shall immediately go over and tell Gnitle's mother all concerning it ; so when Gnitle is again conscious, she may break it to her gently, and when she is able to sit up, I will then take Del over that she may ask Gnitle's forgiveness."

The nurse delivered the message, and Del's mother went over only to find Gnitle still unconscious, and after making known her errand, left feeling very, very sad.

Del, quite the contrary, was all animation, and wanted

to go directly over. Her mother told her it would not do to excite Gnitle; that she might be obliged to wait a number of weeks.

The morning dawned and found her somewhat better. Del seemed delighted, and longed for the time when she would hear of her sitting up

Many weeks passed before she was even able to sit up in bed; but one bright day she seemed stronger than usual, and spoke of Del. Her mother then said "Del is coming over when you are able to sit up, to ask your forgiveness"!

"Then she has confessed! O, I am o glad! Tell her I forgive her, and shall be only too delighted to see her."

From that day she seemed more cheerful, but gained strength slowly. Her faithful grandma, who had noted every change, was rejoicing over each day's improvement, and would sit and tell her stories by the hour. And now as grandma was to have full charge of her during school hours once more, she sought to find whatever would please her most; so to be left with indulgent grandma, greatly pleased Gnitle.

The first day that she sat up in a chair over came Del and her mother. Del ran over to Gnitle, and kissed her, for she knew that she was already forgiven; but Del's mother said "As you have caused Gnitle so much anxiety, and may have been the cause of much of her sickness, it is but right that you go and get down on your knees before her, to show you are truly penitent."

Gladly and humbly she knelt before the one she had wronged, and in a tone of penitence asked to be forgiven; and 'twas a lovely sight to see them join hands in token of friendship once more, their faces beaming with happiness. And too, there were other bright faces in that room. I can assure you. But thinking they would enjoy being left to each other for a short time, all withdrew, and entered into a sprightly conversation in an adjoining room, till Del was ready to leave; then shaking Gnitle's hand, promised to come every day, till she would be able to walk over to see her.

Del was more than true to her promise, as she was over two and three times some days, bringing some delicacy, thinking to tempt Gnitle's appetite. And not a day did she let pass without going to read to Gnitle, and to talk over the pleasant times they would have in the Spring. Who does not look anxiously forward for its joyous return, especially one who has been confined to her room all the Winter? Was it any wonder they talked of row-boats, orchards, swings, etc., and really longed to go hand in hand once more? Each day found them firmer friends than ever; and to this day the unpleasant subject has never been alluded to. All through life they have been brought in contact with each other more or less, and have proved the firmest of friends, and will probably remain so till the end.

That was true forgiveness. That is the way our heavenly Father forgives us when we are truly penitent. He blots everything out, and loves us more and more.

But my little friends, 'tis best to have no secrets to tell, and if you have, don't burden any one with them, for all little girls will not try as Gnitle did to forget them. Very few possess a nature like hers—so sensitive, loving and self sacrificing.

Do you think among your circle of friends there is one who would shield you as Gnitle did Del? Can you think of one that would lie awake night after night, trying to recall the past? Just think of that dear little creature getting out of bed at midnight to write poetry! How plainly those lines show she had been appealing to her Saviour, and had found consolation. The waking up before morning, and the truth flashing across her mind, is proof her prayers were answered.

You will probably think, and perhaps say that her poem does not sound like a child's; nevertheless, I can assure you it was written by Gnitle at midnight, and at the tender age mentioned in the previous chapter. And to convince you more fully that she was a little poetess, I'll give you a poem written by her after the death of her grandma, Gnitle being then about thirteen years old.

After reading the poem, I trust you will read her history with more interest than ever, and conclude poets are born, and that education only lends a charm to their inspirations by polishing the ideas, that they may reflect with brilliancy like the diamond, which if left in its natural state, does not catch the rays of light which render it beautiful and valuable as well. And too, you will find that she really deserved the title of "Sunbeam." So with this explanation, I will now proceed with her poem, dedicated to grandma, which she named

THE OLD ARM CHAIR.

"'The Old Arm Chair
Leave sitting there,
For grandma oft to me did say

'I wonder when I'm far away
If it will old memories bring
Brightly to this household ring.'

"When together
We do gather
It does the dearest and brightest bring.
Whene'er we pray, whene'er we sing,
Grandma's loved voice seems chiming in:
Then why not always count her in?

"This old keepsake
Pray do not take,
But leave it where it ever stood,
For like the ark the flood withstood—
So this old Chair we ne'er can sever,
For it must stand all kinds of weather.

"Grandma's smile
Does oft beguile
And cheer me when I sit alone,
Her pleasant tales and cheerful tone
I hear whene'er my eyes rest there:
Then leave me this—The Old Arm Chair.

"Oft she'd praise me,
Sometimes scold me,
When my little dress I'd tear,
Then kindly add 'My child beware,
When you a nail or brier pass,
If you would be my little lass.'

"Ah, she was kind,
And to my mind
No other voice my heart can cheer,
No other form shall seem so dear,
No other face her smile can wear,
No other one can grace the Chair.

"O, sacred Chair!
A relic there
Till I the stream have safely passed,
And grandma's shore have reached at last:
While time and life's bright visions last,
Let no rude storm the Arm Chair blast."

CHAPTER V.

NOW as we have passed once more through the beautiful gate of Poetry, we will again return to the portal of Prose, hoping it will be open to us again, that we may feel some of the inspiration which actuated "Gnitle, the Sunbeam."

We are not to criticise the efforts of one so young, but we can, and must admit that Gnitle's enthusiasm over grandma, particularly at the close, and in fact throughout the poem, is unbounded, showing how ardent her affection was for her who had always stood by her in sickness and trouble.

She never doubting Gnitle's truthfulness, was one great source of consolation to my little heroine; for it is natural and right that we should love and cherish those who have stood by us in misfortune, or whatever may tend to darken our path through life.

That we may not pass over any portion of her interesting life, we will go back to the Spring succeeding her illness.

While nature was rejoicing, Gnitle seemed to be drooping. Consequently, her physician advised a change of air and scene.

Accordingly, at her mother's suggestion, he took her to board with him in order that she might ride far out in the surrounding country whenever he found it convenient to take her. She was delighted with the idea of having two homes so near together; for said she "When I get tired of one, I can flee to the other; and Del too will always be glad to see me, so that will make three! So you see, grandma, I shall have splendid times"!

"Yes," answered grandma, "I know you will, but what will poor grandma do without you"?

"O I will come hopping in every day to see you, and will have lots of funny things to tell you."

Did ever such a dear little creature live, thought her grandma, as she smiled to think how consoling Gnitle tried to be.

The next morning the doctor called to see whether Gnitle was ready for a drive in the country, and finding she was, took her with him. The doctor's wife being very fond of Gnitle, had often taken her delicacies during her illness; so when Gnitle alighted, and she saw her cheeks rosy once more, said playfully "O Gnitle, why did you paint your cheeks"?

"O just because Mr. Wind and Mr. Sun desired I should look charming when I came in your presence."

"How thoughtful of them. I feel highly complimented. Now if you will go right up to the front room on the right of the hall, and arrange your toilet, we will have dinner immediately."

Up she flew, for the ride had given her an appetite, and in a few minutes was ready to do justice to all that was placed before her. The doctor was much pleased to see her looking so bright and fresh after so long a ride, and told her to be ready early in the morning, as he was going a long distance, aud would require the coolest part of the morning, in order to get back before twelve, as he had several patients to visit in the afternoon.

Just then his little son came bounding in the room, and seeing Gnitle, said "O Nitie! I am so glad you have come. Now I shan't be obliged to go in search of some one to play with me, for we can play ball, and swing, and I guess mother will let us go a fishing. Do you think you could pull me out if I fell in the water"?

"O yes," answered Gnitle, "and a dozen like you"!

"But I would not like to be the last of the dozen."

"All right," said Gnitle, "I will hook you first."

"And sell me for a fish"?

"Yes, if you're not too slippery."

"Why, do you think they would take me for an eel"?

"No, for you would squeal."

"Quite a rhyme," said he.

"Just in time," said she.

"Stop your fooling."

"Don't be ruling."

"At your liking."

Just then a pleasant voice said "If you two are through rhyming, we will go rambling."

"Where"? asked Frank.

"We will leave that to Gnitle."

"O no; it must be left to you."

"Then say we go up the Saw Creek."

Gnitle was very familiar with this stream, so when they had reached the pleasant path, shaded by trees which formed its border, and she saw the large rock in the middle of the stream, she laughed outright, and said:

"One day Del and I stole away to take a bath behind

that rock; but we concluded not to take off our clothing, only our shoes and stockings. Then we skipped from rock to rock, and were far down the stream, where you see the current is very swift. I was showing her a wonderful leap, when down I went, landing on my back, the current carrying me down—down toward the 'deep hole.' All I could hear, except the water, was Del excitedly exclaiming 'O Gnitle! Do try and catch hold of something, or you will land in the 'deep hole.' Well, I did try, and seized a large rock, in which there was a little niche, so I put my hand in this, and with the other caught hold of a little piece that projected, and all at once found myself again on my feet; but the water ran so swiftly, I began to think I would never reach Del again. And when she knew I was safe, she cried for joy, and said, 'O Gnitle, I thought you were lost to me forever.' Yes; and so I began to think. But my time had not come to be drowned, 'and I hope it never will,' said Del. Just the thought of that horrid hole makes me shudder, for people say the bottom has never been reached."

"No wonder," said Frank, "they call it a 'deep hole;' I should call it a 'dead hole.' But Gnitle, you did not tell us what your mother said when you reached home."

"No, you did not give me time. Well, I suppose you think I was punished. No indeed. I did not go home, till my clothes were all dry. We went straight to the cellar kitchen, and Deaun dressed me in some of Del's clothes, while she dried mine. So we said nothing about it then, but sometime after I told my brother, and when I mentioned 'deep hole' he trembled, turned pale, and said: 'A boy, in fun, thinking I could swim, pushed me in, and had not Del's brother, who was an expert swimmer, jumped in and rescued me, I would have gone to the bottom. So Gnitle never let me hear of your going there again"!

"Did you ever tell your mother"?

Frank was anxious to get at that part of the story.

"Yes, but she thought I had been punished enough already, and so only said 'Children should not wander off without their mothers' consent.'"

"Well, I think she was about right," said Frank's mother; "and, my son, I hope you will profit by Gnitle's experience. You have often asked me to let you come here alone, but I, as you know, would not consent. Now, as it is near supper time, we will retrace our steps."

"And sing 'Homeward Bound,'" added Gnitle.

When they reached home they found grandma had been there and brought Gnitle four new spring dresses, some white aprons, and a new pair of shoes.

"O what a good grandma! I must go over to see her to-morrow after the drive," exclaimed Gnitle.

"You are getting homesick," said Frank.

"Not a bit of it," answered Gnitle. Just then the supper bell rang, and all sat down, happy, but tired and hungry.

The doctor left in a hurry, saying, as he drove away, "Go tobed early, Gnitle, so we can be off early in the morning."

After a game at checkers with Frank, Gnitle retired to her room, thinking of—well, I won't say what all, for I do not know.

That reminds me of an old Dutch farmer who used to say: "I do not know"; "I cannot thay"; "but I thay that, and that I thay."

But one thing I do know; that Gnitle was up at break of day, putting on one of her new dresses; and she said, half aloud, "I'm not going to spoil my ride wearing new shoes." Then, taking a look at herself, sat down with a satisfied air thinking how fine she would look in her jaunty hat and well-fitting gloves. For if there was anything Gnitle had a passion for in the line of dress, it was a fashionable hat and close-fitting gloves. Well, there are older people that have the same weakness, if we may call it by that name.

"Now," thought she, "I wish that bell would ring." Just then Frank tapped on the door and sang out "Breakfast"! thinking Gnitle still asleep.

"O I am so glad"! exclaimed Gnitle, opening the door, "for I'm right hungry."

"Yes, but I was only fooling," said Frank, "for I did not think you had risen."

"Did you think I was going to be cheated out of my drive"?

"And the pleasure of wearing a new dress, hat and gloves," added Frank, with a look of admiration. "Come, breakfast is ready, for I hear the bell."

"Ding-dong, ding-dong, we won't be long," said Gnitle as she ran ahead into the dining room, with a happy "good morning" to all.

"Come, all be seated," said the doctor's wife.

After serving him, she asked Gnitle whether it would be milk or coffee.

"Give her coffee this time," said the doctor, "for I'm going to let her drive, so she will have plenty of nerve. While we drive through shady groves I'm going to read my paper."

"And if I should fall asleep and tumble out—oh, my! I shall require two cups of coffee to meet such an emergency," said Gnitle, without giving him time to finish the sentence.

"Yes," said Frank, "better take three."

In a few moments off they drove, the doctor shaking his paper, meaning "wait till we reach a shady grove."

In less than fifteen minutes they were on a road arched over with trees, and wild flowers were springing up as if to give them a welcome.

"When we return," said the doctor, "I will pick some of these little beauties to take home with us." Then handing Gnitle the reins, with a smile, began reading his paper.

Taking the reins always pleased Gnitle, for she was well able to hold and manage them, too. Once she thought she saw the doctor nod.

"O," she said, "I wish I had brought a flask of coffee."

The doctor, taking the hint, laughingly said "I guess we won't need it to-day.

When they reached the highway, the doctor took the reins, and hurried along till they reached the house of his boy patient, who was suffering from hip trouble.

After tying his horse to a large shady tree, he told Gnitle to remain there in the cool air and read a little book he had brought to amuse her. It being full of pictures and stories, Gnitle did not find even time to brush the big horse-flies away.

Gnitle had said when the doctor left her, "I can keep the flies away, too." And he made answer, "Look out lest they take you with them."

In a few moments the doctor very kindly brought out a

glass of water to Gnitle. "O, thank you! This is far better than coffee," said she, mischievously, as she handed him the glass.

"Yes, so it is. Now you can read your book a short time longer, or, if you choose, take a short walk; perhaps you would feel rested and better able to handle the reins while I pick flowers."

In a very short time they were driving homeward; Gnitle watched with longing eyes for the beautiful grove they were soon to enter, where they would be sheltered from the burning sun and free from dust. When they reached the entrance, the doctor alighted to pick wild flowers, while Gnitle with great delight drove slowly through the forest.

As the doctor approached the carriage, Gnitle exclaimed "How many, and so beautiful. Why, they will last a week if I cut off the stems and give them fresh water every day."

The doctor replied, "I see you understand the art of preserving them, so you had better take charge of the flowers and I'll take the reins. I think we will reach home just in time for dinner."

Soon as they reached home, out came Frank to help Gnitle alight; and when he spied the flowers he almost forgot to assist her in his eagerness to seize them.

"O Frank," said Gnitle, "I wish you could have been with us, but I'll not take time to tell you now; so run quickly and get me some water lest they wither."

"O let me fly thither," said Frank, "and bring it hither."

"Lest they wither," added Gnitle.

"Rhyming again," exclaimed Frank, after putting the flowers in a large, old-fashioned vase. He then started to see if dinner was ready, returning in a moment, sang out—

"Come to dinner, little sinner! Now beat that, if you can," exclaimed Frank. "I shall do no more rhyming till I'm through dining."

"What a fib! What do you call that? Chicken pot-pie —just what I like," answered Gnitle, as she had already smelled some of its delightful odor.

A pot-pie dinner tends to put little folks in good humor.

"Now, Frank," said Gnitle as she took her glass of milk, "I'll drink your health, and wish you wealth."

"I will return the compliment, but only wish you wealth, for I think you have health enough."

"Yes, and I shall (if I take her driving many times) charge extra for each meal after a drive," said the doctor, winking knowingly at his wife. "To-morrow I shall drive over a rough and hilly road; so, Frank, if you are up bright and early, I will take you for a shake up. It does bad boys good to shake them."

"Yes," answered Gnitle, taking up the joke; "my mama says if boys received more shakings and whippings there would not be so many people hung."

This made them all laugh, Frank remarking at the same time "Gnitle's 'goodness' is now all accounted for."

"If you think so, why not experiment on you"?

"Perhaps mother has tried it already, and found the result not satisfactory," said Frank, with a roguish look as Gnitle hurried away to visit her mother, grandma and sister. She had only been away from them two nights, but to them it seemed a week or more. They called her their "Sunbeam," and were looking anxiously for the little bright face to enter. They did not wait long, when to surprise them, Gnitle tapped on the door.

"O you little mischief," said her sister; "what did you tap for"?

"O just for the fun of making you run. Where is mama, and grandma"?

"Here we are; you made us run, too, as we were not prepared to receive any but you."

"Why, I only tapped to have a little fun."

"We'll excuse you this time, so sit down and tell us how you are pleased with your new home."

"O I have delightful times. The doctor and his wife are so pleasant, and Frank so comical. To-day when I came home she had made a chicken pot-pie, just because she knew I was fond of it. How kind of her, and how good it tasted after so long a drive."

"Well, I hope you will always be ready to oblige her, and never give her unnecessary trouble, lest she tire of you or think you selfish," said her mother. "Ride whenever you can, as it will give you an appetite, and thus you will gain strength and be ready to commence school again in the Fall. You will be obliged to assist me at times, as I intend to send your sister away to school that she may study French, Latin and Music. So try and get your strength, for I shall need your assistance. Your sister was about your age when she took charge of some of the classes."

"O I will make a splendid little teacher. Yes, and make them understand me, too."

"I hope you will be able to explain, for in this consists the true method of teaching. Many highly educated people have not this faculty. To be able to impart our knowledge to others is a wonderful gift—a precious gift—

one that will make thousands happy besides ourselves; and that is what we should live for."

"O mama, you would make a splendid lecturer; but I will come again soon and give you a chance to finish. I will now thank grandma for the new dresses, etc., then run over to see Del. So good-by for the present."

Del was standing at the gate waiting for her to pass.

"I was afraid you had gone home without my seeing you, as I wish you to come over to-morrow, bright and early, to spend the day."

"All right, I shall be most happy to do so; but I must go now, as supper is waiting my return."

"O you little runaway," said Frank. "Come out to supper; then we will have a game at ball."

Having finished this delightful game, they walked to the house hand-in-hand, talking over the happy times both anticipated.

"We must retire early," said Frank, "or I shall be left, for I fear I may oversleep myself."

"Yes, and will you take your fishing-pole"?

"Think I will, now that you have reminded me, for I can take a stroll up the creek while father visits his patient."

"Do be careful," said Gnitle, "for when we are not accustomed to a stream, there is often danger we cannot foresee."

"I know it, and why you are so timid."

"Yes, I have very good reason to be afraid of the water."

"But, you know, little boats should keep near shore, while larger ones can venture more."

"Well, well! Did you have to warn me by way of rhyme lest I might forget it"?

"Now, as it is nearly nine, I'll go, and lose no time."

"So will I; come, let's fly," said Gnitle. And away they scampered, saying, "I'll be the first one up."

The next morning both popped into the dining room at the same time, full of glee.

"Well," remarked the doctor, "you both look very mischievous. I think a shaking-up would be of great benefit to both."

"Yes, but we can't all ride; one of us might tumble out and get one shake too many. Besides, I am going to spend the day with Del. So, Frank, if you get back early, come to Del's, and we will row out in the channel."

"Yes, and I'll bring a string of fish, so Deaun can cook my supper."

"Well, I'll tell her; she's a good old soul, and always ready to oblige."

After seeing the doctor and Frank drive away, Gnitle bade the doctor's wife good morning, and hastened to make the promised visit.

Del had been watching for her; so, taking her hand, ran over to say "good morning" to the folks at home. They were soon back, and Del's mama kissed Gnitle, and was delighted to see her looking so well.

Gnitle thanked her for such an agreeable compliment, for Gnitle, like most people, liked to be told she was look ing well.

She then started to tell Deaun what Frank had said concerning the fish.

"Bless you, childer, I would fry all de fish dat am in de

brook for such a sweet little lassie," said Deaun, showing her big white teeth the while.

"Now come," said Del, "we must have some fun. I have a splendid new jumping rope; let's see how fast we can jump."

This being pretty warm work, they soon tired, and ran for the swing. Finding this cooler exercise, they remained in it some time, talking and laughing as in days of yore. Finally both started for the orchard, where they refreshed themselves with johnny apples. Perhaps you may not know them by this name. They are little, and red on both sides, sour savored with sweet, like vinegar with sugar added; we will call them a sweet-sour, and add they are delicious—at least Del and Gnitle thought so.

After feasting awhile on apples, they concluded to stroll up the Saw Creek.

"Now don't be jumping in there again," said Del.

"No need of caution," answered Gnitle, laughing. "I begin to feel tired, and I rather think 'tis dinner time. Yes, for there goes farmer Dow and his men. Their big dinner horn must have blown."

As they reached the gate, there stood Frank with a new suit of clothes on.

"Well, Frank," said Gnitle, "I expected to see fish, instead of a new suit."

"Well, you would have seen a pretty one about two hours ago, for I tumbled in and had to borrow this suit. It happened father's patient was about my size, or I would have had to hung myself out to dry. No clothing establishment within ten miles."

'My warning did not save you then."

"No, but a man did by jumping in after me."

"How lucky you were to have the man so near."

"Yes, indeed, and father says when he visits his patient again, I must take him a valuable present. I think it will be a handsome watch."

"I was just going to say that would be a useful present, and probably one he would appreciate," added Gnitle. "I hardly think you will care to take a sail."

"No, I have seen enough water for one day. Dry land will please me better."

"Like Christopher Columbus and his crew, I could have cried "Land! land"!

"Won't a little dinner please you better still"? said Del. "I know it will me."

"And me, too," answered Gnitle. Then in they marched to dinner.

"Well, my boy, where am de fish"?

"O, I left them in the creek, and was only too glad to get out myself."

"T'ank de Lord you did, so neber mind de fish; but me got de fat and ebery t'ing ready, Mither Frank."

"Thank you, Deaun, but the dinner is so very nice, I don't care for fish, especially when I have been so recently in their company.

This remark made Deaun exclaim "Yah, yah, yah"!

She had spread the table for these little folks so they could enjoy being alone. And what a deliciously spread table it was. Everything that little girls and boys are sure to like was on it; and I can assure you the "goodies" disappeared rapidly. Meanwhile, keeping up a sprightly conversation, Deaun putting in a word now and then, feeling privileged, being an old servant, and very fond of the children.

About an hour had been taken up eating this delightful meal.

"Now," said Frank, "come, I have brought my ball; let's have a short game out on the lawn."

"All right," said Del, "two to catch it and one to knock it, so give me the club."

"Are clubs trumps, the reason you want it"?

"I'll make it trumps or give that ball thumps, if I don't hit it, and send it over the pond," said Del.

Sure enough, Del sent it flying, not over, but into the pond.

"Now," said Frank, "we'll all jump into the boat and sail for it."

They were soon in pursuit, and trying which could grab it first.

"O here it is," said Gnitle. "Seems to me this is a great day for pulling out."

"I think as much," said Del, and Frank laughed outright.

"Give us your hand, Gnitle, for you hold the trump this time. Now we will row back, for I feel somewhat tired."

"And would avoid being pulled out again," said Gnitle, smiling. "Suppose we sit quietly under the willow for a short time."

"All right, that will just suit me," said Frank; "for, to be frank, I am very tired."

"So are we. Now please entertain us by telling how you managed to fall in the water."

"Why, the easiest you ever saw. I was jumping from

rock to rock—the stream being low—and had just taken my seat on a large one in order to drop my line, when in rushed the tide, carrying me and pole down among the finny tribe. I clung to the pole, thinking it might be an assistance, but soon let it go and tried to swim. I was making a great effort, when a hand seized me by the coat collar. 'See here, boy, what are you trying to do'? said the man. You would have soon been beyond my reach. When I get you on shore I will show you what danger you have escaped. Now,' said he, 'follow me a few steps and I will show you. Do you see that white foam? Well, you would have soon plunged into it, and no mortal power could have saved you.' As we walked back we met father. He seeing me so wet, soon realized what had happened. So, after thanking the man, told him he would not forget him, and then hurried along to get dry clothes for me. Now I have told you all, so if you will excuse me, I will take my departure. I feel the need of rest. Besides, mother said 'Don't tarry long.'"

"I am sorry to have you leave before supper, but I suppose you know your own feelings best," said Del.

"Yes, and mother's, too. Go, by all means; I would not have you disobey her," said Gnitle, "she is such a dear, good mother."

"Good by; come home early, won't you, Gnitle"?

"Yes; I will not stay late. Del and I will run over home a short time, for I know they all miss me very much. Poor grandma looks so lonesome when I leave her; I know she will be glad to have me home again."

"Don't you think we will miss you, too"? said Frank, as he turned to leave.

"I hope so, but I'm afraid nobody will cry after me," said Gnitle, with a roguish look. "Now come, Del, let's go over to see the folks."

They soon entered, full of glee; Gnitle, seated on grandma's knee, was trying to console her over the loss of an old pet cat which had made grandma feel rather sad.

"Never mind," said Gnitle, "I will soon come and more than fill her place."

"Well, well"! said grandma, laughing, "I hope you don't put yourself on the same footing with the cat."

Just then her mama came in and kissed them.

"O," said she; "Gnitle, how healthy you look. Fall will soon be here, so ride all you can. In two weeks more I shall expect you home."

"All right, mama; and Del will come over to tea the day I return. So good-by for the present. Del's supper will be waiting our return."

Supper being over, Gnitle tarried a short time, keeping her promise—for in this she was very prompt—and Del walked home with her. When they reached the gate, she said "I shall be only too glad when I can leave you at your real home."

"And will you be glad to march off to school again"?

"Of course I will, so long as you are going, too."

"I like to hear you say so, for I shall be ready when school opens. Tell Frank to be ready to shoulder his books, too," said Del, as she turned to go back.

"O I'll be ready," exclaimed Frank (happening to overhear them; boys never listen—no, never), "for you know we are going to have a new teacher"—meaning Gnitle.

"Yes, and I'll make you walk the chalk-line, too," said Gnitle.

"Won't she be strict. O, I'm so afraid. I tremble already," jestingly said Frank.

"When Gnitle entered, the doctor's wife called her, and said "See what I've selected for Frank's life preserver." Whereupon she brought out a beautiful watch with "W. S. D." engraved on the back. "To-morrow Frank, you must go and present it. When the minute hand is nearly to eleven, I would like you to point to it and say 'Father says as you did not wait till the eleventh hour to perform a noble action, he could not wait till then to reward one; so please accept this as an expression of his gratitude.'"

"That will be a beautiful way to present it," said Gnitle, "but *his* seems rather selfish; suppose we change it thus, and say *our* gratitude."

Frank and his father were off bright and early the next morning. When they reached the house of his patient, Frank went in and thanked them for their kindness, put on his own clothes, and then walked to the gentleman's house. He found him standing in the yard.

"Ah, my boy," said he, "I did not know you in dry clothes! I hope you did not take cold."

"No, sir," answered Frank. Then opening the watch, and finding it lacked just a quarter of eleven, he pointed to the hand, and presented it to the gentleman as he was told.

"Thank you," said the gentleman, glancing at the time. "This will serve to remind me of you morning and night, and the watch will always be a memento I shall hold as an expression of gratitude."

Frank then shook his hand warmly, and asked him to pay them a visit.

"Thank you," replied the gentleman, "and I shall always be happy to have you visit me."

Frank left, saying to himself "What a perfect gentleman. What a beautiful answer."

"Well, Frank," said the doctor, "did you find the gentleman in"?

"Yes, sir, and I found him a perfect one, too. It wanted fifteen minutes of eleven when I presented the watch. Looking at the time he said 'This will remind me of you morning and night, and the watch will serve as a memento of gratitude.' Wasn't that a beautiful and appropriate answer"?

"Yes, my son; it convinces me that he possesses fine feelings and very quick perception. Did you ask him to come and see us"?

"Yes, sir; he thanked me, and said he should always be happy to have me visit him."

"You must, and so will I," said the doctor, looking somewhat happier than on the previous day.

Gnitle was anxiously awaiting their arrival.

"Here we are," said the doctor, "safe and sound. Is dinner ready? If it is, I won't unhitch my horse till I see one more patient. It will be a pleasant drive, so if you are ready, Gnitle, you may accompany me."

While they were at dinner, Frank entertained them talking about the true gentleman he had so accidently met.

"You see," said Frank's mother, "he acted well his part; in that the honor lies. See that you try to be just as ready and gentlemanly; it will gain you many friends."

" Now, mother, if you are through with him, I'll set him at the business at once. So just help Gnitle into the carriage ; that will be one way to commence, for we must go step by step ; then it comes perfectly natural. Now you can hand me my whip, and that will be another step. Next you can close the gate after us. Then we will thank you and let you rest till we return, and then you can help Gnitle alight."

" Clever," said Frank, smiling, as they drove off.

The two weeks had slipped around and Gnitle was preparing to leave her adopted home (as she called it) for her real one once more.

Breakfast being over, the doctor's wife called Gnitle in the sitting room. Smiling as usual, Gnitle came in.

" You need not look so happy because you are going to leave us, for I feel very sad to part with you, and wish—but it is wicked to covet, so I will say no more, only that I hope you will come and see me often."

" I certainly shall, for I cannot forget how kind you have been during my illness, and since I have been with you. So have the doctor and Frank done all they could for my health and happiness."

" Poor Frank, how he will miss you."

" We will meet at school, and he will have his time occupied with lessons," answered Gnitle, by way of consolation. " I shall be very busy helping mama during school hours. My sister will not be there to help, so I shall be obliged to take her place," said Gnitle, looking somewhat proud.

" You will make quite a young teacher, but I think you will be a good and patient one."

"I fear not very patient with the dumb ones, but I will try."

After dinner the doctor called Gnitle, and said—

"Now, my little girl, get ready and I'll take you home in my carriage. When I brought you here you were pale and sickly; now I'm going to take you back plump and rosy. Now, Frank, bring down the little trunk. That will be another way of showing your usefulness, and then you can politely assist Gnitle in the carriage."

"Good-by," softly said the doctor's wife, her eyes filling with tears as she kissed her. "But," she added, "you'll remember to come and see me often."

"Most assuredly I will, for it will be only too great a pleasure," answered Gnitle.

"I'll not say good-by," said Frank, "for I'm to have supper with you and Del."

CHAPTER VI.

THEY were soon at the gate, where they were welcomed by Gnitle's mother and Del. After commenting on the great improvement the change had made in Gnitle, she thanked the doctor, for she felt money could never pay for all the gratitude she felt that he was entitled to for his kind and assiduous care over Gnitle. She then helped her from the carriage, saying as she did so—

"O my, Gnitle, how many pounds you must have gained."

"Yes, and bright eyes and rosy cheeks, too," added grandma.

"And," said the doctor, shaking her plump little hand, "you must try to retain them by taking plenty of exercise in the open air."

"Thank you, I will certainly take your advice, for it is far easier to take than medicine, I find," answered Gnitle, as he waived his hand and drove away.

"O Del! I am so glad you are already here. Frank will be here too, and we will have the table all to ourselves, can we not, grandma"?

"Yes, and the dining-room, too, if it's your wish. And what would you like for supper"?

"Hot biscuits, jelly cake, chocolate drops, smoked beef, cheese, plum preserves, and a glass of milk."

"All right," said grandma, "the cake was made this morning; the other things are in the house, and the biscuits shall be nice and hot. Now go and entertain your company, and I'll have everything in apple-pie order."

"O here comes Frank," said Del, "bringing a basket which seems quite heavy."

Gnitle ran to him and caught hold of the basket, peeping in at the same time.

"Here, here, none of that! these were sent to your mother."

"O what a nice present! See here, mama, what Frank has brought you."

"O thank you," exclaimed Gnitle's mother, taking the basket, "I'm afraid it has made your little arms ache," as she emptied its contents.

"Such beautiful green-gages; do look, grandma," said Gnitle.

"Yes, and I'll stew some for supper," added grandma.

The three now bound for a frolic, started off, saying "What shall we do first"?

"Let's go down to the saw mill and jump the logs," said Frank.

This was great fun, and I will tell you how it was done. The one that leaped over the remaining log last was obliged to tag all the rest, and if not successful the first time going over, he or she was expected to go till this wonderful feat had been accomplished. This was great fun for the litte folks, don't you think so? "Yes, yes," I hear you say, "so it is, and wouldn't I like to have been one of that little party."

The logs were only a short distance apart on the green

which occupied a large space in front of the mill, the grass rendering it soft and velvety to little feet. Bright eyes, rosy cheeks, and a good appetite were sure to follow such lively play. You would have thought so if you could have seen the hot biscuits disappear, while grandma kept the plate replenished.

"What shall we do when we are through supper"?

"Look for four-leaved clover," said Del, "and make a wish over the first one we find."

"I'll put mine in a book and press them," said Frank.

"Then you expect to find more than one, do you"?

"Sometimes I find several, and I have found them with five and six leaves," said Frank.

"I'm going to put mine under my pillow to see what I will dream," was Gnitle's reply.

"If you do I hope you will dream the old scratch is after you," said Frank. "It would serve you right."

All pushed back their chairs and started in quest. After looking some time and finding none, they concluded this was dull amusement, so they went over to Del's to jump the rope. Del's little sister Nenie and Gnitle turned the rope while Del and Frank played "chase the fox." You know, I presume, how this is done. One tries to catch the other while going through.

"It is now time for me to run home, so I'll go over and get my basket," said Frank, extending his hands to both at the same time. Then shaking their hands heartily, and with a very roguish look, he said "I suppose we shall all meet in the school-room on Monday."

"Yes," answered Del, "but I pity the new teacher with such customers as we are to deal with."

"O," said Gnitle, taking up the joke, "you had better extend your sympathy to the latter. We will see when Monday comes who'll need it. You'll find it won't be me," she said, as he ran over to get his basket and to bid them good afternoon.

"I suppose if nothing prevents, I shall see you at school opening day"? said Gnitle's mother.

"O certainly," said Frank, taking his departure. Seeing Gnitle at the gate he shook his fingers at her, meaning—"Look out for Monday." For he could not help thinking how funny it would be to have Gnitle for a teacher.

Sunday they all met at Sabbath-school. Even there Frank wore the same mischievous look whenever he chanced to catch Gnitle's eye.

Monday came, and off marched the little teacher with all the dignity imaginable, roll-book in hand, ready to call the names when the scholars were assembled. Well, if you could have seen the stately little creature as she mounted the platform and tapped with her rule on the desk. The children were too much surprised to think of being disorderly, so they answered to their names just as though nothing unusual had occurred, while Del and Frank looked at each other in blank amazement.

Having called the roll, she tapped again for each one to give immediate attention while she read from the Bible the chapter commencing "Children, obey your parents in the Lord, for this is right. Honor thy father and mother, which is the first commandment with promise."

"Now can any little boy or girl repeat the promise"? asked the stately little teacher.

Up rose Frank and Del, much to Gnitle's surprise.

"You ma rc, ert it together, if you please," sai l Gnitle, (oking ver grave.

After the ' ad done so, she ' ad t' e scholars repeat it in concert.

"As some of you may have forgotton what the promise is, I will remind you—'That it may be well with thee, and thou mayest be long lived upon earth.'" She then added: "these words you will find in the sixth chapter of Ephesians, sixth and third verses. What a beautiful promise," said Gnitle. "Now, listen attentively, for I may ask you another question before I am through, and shall expect some one to answer. 'Does God promise to reward us for the good we do here'"?

"Yes, ma'am," answered the scholars.

"Can any of you repeat the eighth verse"?

They seemed to have forgotten the commencement, so she started them by giving them the first word. They then repeated the verse without hesitation. If I should give you, my readers, the first word of the verse, do you think you could repeat it? "Knowing" is the word, so try, and if you find you cannot, do not wait, but get your Bible immediately. It is a precious and beautiful promise—one full of inspiration—one that should make us ever anxious to do good to those around us, and to the stranger as well, whenever it lies in our power to aid any such.

While they were repeating this beautiful passage, Gnitle's mother entered the school room.

After complimenting them for their good behavior, she told them she had been unavoidably detained, and hoped, if such should occur again, to find them always as orderly as then. The children all looked delighted, and so did

Gnitle. And from that day every child in the school looked upon her as something more than ordinary, and consequently entertained for her the h'ghest respect.

She had made a lasting impression at first on their youthful minds, and in so doing she had laid the foundation on which to build success. Thus through life it had been Gnitle's aim to make a favorable impression, and as her lot has been cast among strangers, to a great extent, more than she ever anticipated, she has found it the source of great pleasure to be able to please and interest them at once. She consequently holds to the belief that "first impressions are always lasting." I think it quite true, not only in regard to people, but in dwellings as well. For instance: if a house is surrounded by beautiful flowers and wide, grassy lawns, we receive a bright impression. If we enter a hall and find it dark, gloomy and dusty, we certainly are not impressed favorably. Gnitle would say "Mama, if ever I have a house of my own, I am going to have my hall furnished just as handsomely as my means will allow, and it shall always be cleanly and cheerful." "Yes, my dear, and let this cleanly and cheerful appearance extend to your doors and windows as well, for they, to the passer-by, speak in a silent but plain language not to be misunderstood."

Now as we have dwelt longer than I expected on Gnitle's favorite theme, we will return to the school-room, where we left Gnitle, her mother, and all so happy.

The mother has resumed charge, and has sent out the first, or highest class, which she superintends, while Gnitle has charge of those remaining in larger rooms. To some, tl. .vould have been a difficult task, but not so was it for

Gnitle ; for while she was hearing a class read or spell, the others were writing on slates or copy-books, while those more advanced were ciphering out difficult problems in arithmetic. When she was through, this class took their seats quietly to do whatever was assigned them, and the next would take their place. The pupils were always expected to stand while reading or reciting a lesson. In that way they did not tire between intermissions. They were allowed twenty minutes in the forenoon, an hour at noon, and fifteen minutes in the afternoon for recreation. While they were at play, Gnitle examined the copy-books, while her mother mended the pens. Then they wrote with a goose-quill, so it was necessary to make and mend the pens, which took too much time during school hours.

"When did Gnitle study"? methinks I hear you ask. After school she took a walk, or called to see some absent scholar or intimate friend ; then she would return and study, so as to recite her lessons in the evening to her mother. In this way she kept up with the class, and oftentimes being instructed the night previous in some particular lesson, she was competent, and relieved her mother by taking charge of the highest class, too. This rendered it easier for both, as using the voice constantly is tiresome and injurious.

As the copies for the first class took no small amount of time, and finding rest through this change, it stimulated Gnitle to study in order that she might give her mother all the rest from teaching she possibly could, for while seated at her desk the pupils under her charge wrote or ciphered. Thus day after day Gnitle and her mother toiled together. It was not unpleasant toil to them, for they were never happier than when in the school-room. It seemed to be a part of their nature, for they were heart and soul in it, and the children seemed to imbibe the same spirit ; for none seemed anxious to leave, but would wait till the school-house door had been safely locked before they were inclined to travel homeward.

Del and Frank were so charmed with Gnit'e's first appearance on that eventful Monday, that no eulogy was sufficient to express their praise, and so gave vent to their thoughts by saying "Gnitle is no humbug, but a genuine teacher." And Frank, when he reached home, exclaimed, "O mother, I felt just like having some fun when I found her mother not there ; but when I looked around and saw the others so orderly, and she so dignified, I thought of what you said the day I returned from that gentleman's dwelling—'So acted well my part.'"

"I am pleased to hear you say so, and hope you will profit by his and likewise by her example ; for of all little girls I ever knew, she is the most polite and thoughtful. When you return, tell her to call on me very soon, as I am anxious to see her."

While walking back to school he chanced to overtake Del.

"Did you ever see anything to beat it"? said Frank.

"No, never ; I think she could command a regiment," answered Del.

"She was cut out for a teacher, that's very evident," said Frank.

"Come, we must run, or we'll be late," said Del.

But they were in time, and Frank delivered his mother's message.

"Thank you," said Gnitle, "tell her I will call very soon. But say to her that I not only study after school, but teach, too ; for mama has taken the lady's daughter with whom my sister boards, by way of exchange, to educate. On account of previous ill-health, our pupil is somewhat backward, consequently we shall be obliged to give her extra lessons for a time, that she may regain what she has lost ; so we intend to be very thorough with her, that she may soon be in the highest class."

"And does your sister feel at home there"?

"Yes, and will remain till she graduates."

There the conversation ended, it being time for the scholars to assemble.

The next afternoon she made a call on Frank's mother.

She was only too delighted to see Gnitle, and complimented her great success as a teacher, and invited her to stay to supper. Gnitle said she would like very much to stay, but had promised her mother to return in an hour, to assist the new pupil to study and prepare her lessons for the morrow.

"Gnitle, I am afraid you are over-taxed," said the doctor's wife.

"I love to teach," answered Gnitle, not dreaming how soon she would be obliged to be only a scholar again. Gnitle did not know all that was transpiring at home. And just as well she did not.

One day she saw Mr. Whenford, a widower, take her mother for a drive, after which he put his horse in the barn, took supper, and spent the evening. He had frequently called on her grandma and taken supper with them, so Gnitle was reconciled to all but the drive. That was something out of the general order.

Gnitle's mother had been a widow so long it did not occur to Gnitle that she might, or ever would marry, till he made his appearance again on Sunday evening. When she saw him again in the parlor, it roused her suspicion that there might be other motives than friendship. Well, if you could have seen her run for her grandma, you would have laughed or pitied her, but I think the latter. She had a mild, brown eye, but it flashed with something other than mildness then.

"O," said she, "grandma, that horrid fellow is here again."

"Hush," said grandma, "he will hear you."

"I don't care if he does; and I'm going to take my seat in the parlor, and am not going to leave it till he goes."

"O," said grandma, "that would not be ladylike, and it would make you appear saucy."

"Can't help that; this is rushing matters too much," said Gnitle, still standing with a look of firm resolution.

"Sit down, child, I want to talk with you."

"I don't feel like talking; I'm going to take my seat in the parlor."

"Come here, Gnitle, you would not do such a foolish thing," said grandma.

"Well, if he stays a minute after nine I shall."

Grandma had a little foot-stool under her feet, which she pushed forward for her to sit on. Gnitle sat down on it, and put her head in grandma's lap, and cried as if her little heart would break.

"Why you foolish child," said grandma, stroking her hair.

"I don't think I'm half so foolish as mama would be to marry again, now that we are all able to help ourselves and her, too."

"Perhaps she has no such thoughts," said grandma, trying to soothe her.

"Perhaps not," replied Gnitle, a little sarcastically. "And if she does, I shall tell her my mind freely."

"I'm sure you always seemed to like him."

"Well, I have nothing against him personally, but just think of mama going in that large family. Hasn't she had care enough already? And I'm just getting so I can assist her."

"Yes, dear, I know you are a great help to her, but she will soon be too old to teach, and in a year or two you will be sent away to school, and poor grandma can't live always; then she will have some one to cheer her. Besides, she would not be far away—only two miles, just think. We could almost walk to see her."

"You walk so far"! That made Gnitle laugh. Then she added, "I guess there would be no need of your walking, for he would be only too delighted to come after you. But, Grandma, I do hope we may all remain together. Any way, I shall never leave you," said Gnitle, with tears in her eyes.

"No, child, I hope you never will have occasion to, for I missed you so much the short time you boarded with the doctor."

"Yes, but did I not come to see you nearly every day"?

"Yes, but still I felt your absence very much. One

thing you may rest assured of, that I shall never consent to your leaving me, unless it is to go away to school. But as that is looking ahead two years at the least, we won't be thinking of that now."

"No, for we have something else to think of now," said Gnitle, with meaning in her tone. Then drawing a deep sigh, she looked steadily at the parlor door. She took her seat on the little foot-stool again, and began to question grandma.

"Now, grandma, do you think mama will ever do such a foolish thing"?

"My child, I don't consider she would be taking a foolish step. I married twice, and I never had cause to regret it, and I don't see any reason why she should, for he is certainly very talented. I don't wish to hear a better sermon than he can preach, and he has a beautiful home and a farm of two hundred acres, with everything desirable growing upon it—fine cattle, fowls of all kinds, eight big fat hogs ready to kill, and a beef; besides, he has two field horses to perform the labor, and a splendid span of bays, which he drives for pleasure. Now, what could she desire more"? said grandma, thinking to console Gnitle.

"O, grandma, don't talk to me any more in that way, for it only makes me angry," said Gnitle, glancing at the clock. "There, it is after nine and he hasn't gone yet."

"Yes, but he'll soon go, for he never keeps late hours."

"Well, I wish he would spend his hours and minutes somewhere else besides here," answered Gnitle, putting her hand to her head. "Dear, dear! I never had anything make me feel like this."

"Yes, but perhaps you are giving yourself unnecessary anxiety. Never worry over anything imaginary."

Thus grandma tried to console her, but she found it a difficult task. Gnitle constantly glanced at the clock. Each minute to her seemed an hour.

Finally, when the hour hand had reached eleven and the clock was striking, she jumped up like one electrified, and darted for the door; but as she put her hand on the knob, her courage seemed to fail her, and again she took her seat in front of grandma, saying—

"O, I wish he would go. Never mind, let him go when he gets ready; we won't care."

"Yes, I do care, and wish him to Balhack," said grandma, trying to soothe her.

As laughing was quite out of the question, Gnitle smiled faintly and said "I wish I could go to sleep."

A few moments after grandma went into the kitchen to take a small pill of opium which the doctor had ordered her to take every other night.

Gnitle seeing her swallow it, said "Do make one for me, too," and then threw herself into an old-fashioned cradle, in which grandma had often rocked her.

Of course grandma prepared a pill the size of a pin's head, biting her lips to keep from laughing the while. Then putting it into Gnitle's hand, she told her to swallow it and lie down, then she would rock her to sleep.

Gnitle looked at the little pill, saying as she did so, "This isn't half large enough."

"O, yes it is," answered grandma, "and you'll be asleep before you know it. Come, swallow it quickly, then lie down"—handing her at the time a glass of water.

Seeing grandma appeared in earnest, she did so, and soon fell asleep. But I rather think grandma's rocking took effect before the pill. Be that as it may, grandma felt quite relieved when she found she had really gone to sleep, and hoped that she would not wake up till the widower had departed.

When she heard the street door close she said "Thankful am I the child is still asleep." She then told her daughter how excited Gnitle had been throughout the evening. It made her feel very sad, but when grandma told her about the pill, she could not refrain from laughing; neither could grandma.

"Where is she now"? asked the mother.

"Still asleep in the cradle, and it is best to let her remain there till she awakens. I will cover her warmly, so she will take no cold," said grandma as she left the room.

Gnitle slept till four o'clock in the morning. Not seeing grandma, she arose, went to the parlor door, and listened. Finding all quiet, she walked noiselessly, and crawled as far back in the bed as possible. Her mother appeared to take no notice of it, as she did not wish to excite her more, knowing the cause of this coolness.

In the morning she was uncommonly gracious to Gnitle; but Gnitle remained extremely cool, paying all attention to grandma. She ate very little breakfast, but did not forget to be polite to the new pupil, telling her not to follow her example in regard to eating, as she did not feel well.

Soon they were on their way to school, where they were met by Frank and Del.

"What is the matter, Gnitle? You don't look well," said Del.

"Don't feel so," said Gnitle, taking her seat at the desk to avoid showing her emotion.

All that day she found teaching an arduous duty. Absentmindedness seemed to characterize everything she did. When she should have called out the reading class, it was geography instead. Thus she blundered, causing some confusion. But as there was no one but the scholars to witness it, she only smiled and said "Never mind, you know I don't feel well to-day."

"Well, come and sit down, then perhaps you may soon feel better."

Gnitle did not take her walk after school, but went to her room and there remained there till supper time, thinking over matters, and trying to reconcile herself to whatever change might be in store for them.

"For," thought she, "mama will not listen to poor little me, when so many older ones sacntion it. Just think," reasoned Gnitle, "of all his folks being in favor of the union, and I know grandma, aunt, sister and brother will not oppose it ; so I will be obliged to battle alone. Well, I'm going to speak my mind freely ; I'm not going to give it up so ; but I suppose it will be like Job contending with the Almighty."

While she was thus reasoning, her mother and grandma were consulting as to the best course to pursue with Gnitle.

"Be straightforward with her," said grandma ; "that is the only way to manage Gnitle."

Just then Julia (the new pupil) entered without Gnitle

"Where did you leave Gnitle"? asked grandma, thinking they had gone out together.

"Gnitle went to lie down, thinking it might ease her head," answered Julia.

"I did not know she was suffering from headache, so if you will go up and tell her grandma has a cup of tea for her, I will be greatly obliged."

Julia went and tapped lightly on the door, but receiving no answer, she returned, saying "she must have fallen asleep."

Grandma went to her daughter's room feeling much excited.

"That poor child has gone to bed with heartache, and not headache, as Julia has been led to think, and after supper you must talk with her, and not keep her in suspense."

"Yes, I have been thinking that would be the best course," said the mother.

Supper being ready, Gnitle presented herself.

"Do you feel better"? asked Julia.

"Yes, but I'm not hungry," said Gnitle, taking her seat at the table.

Her mother seeing she ate very little, and noticing how quiet and dejected she was, pitied her, and said, as she arose from the table—

"Gnitle, come up to my room presently; I wish to see you a few moments."

Gnitle did as requested, and when she entered, her mother took her by the hand, saying "Gnitle, grandma has told me that you were not pleased with Mr. W——'s calling here on Sunday evening."

"No, nor did I like his taking you for a drive", answered Gnitle very resolutely.

"Now, my child, don't worry any more about Mr. W———, for you know he is an old friend, and when I receive him in any other light, you and grandma will be the first to know it. Now go, and don't worry if he should chance to call occasionally, for I will not keep anything from you."

Gnitle seemed greatly relieved. She kissed her mother, and then went to grandma, looking very happy. Grandma remarked the change in her appearance, and suggested a short walk before studying her lessons.

"I will; so come, Julia," said Gnitle, "we can study our lessons this evening, and recite them all before half-past nine. Let us take a stroll up the creek, for this fine weather will not last much longer, so let's enjoy it."

And over they went for Del.

"O, I was just wishing you would come," said Del, "for I feel just like walking."

Then the three marched off together. When they returned, Gnitle said she felt as if some supper would taste good.

"Your walk has made you hungry, so both come out and have some supper," said grandma.

Julia did not refuse, for she felt hungry too, seeing Gnitle again so bright and happy.

"How true it is, 'the heart is light when all is bright,'" thought Gnitle and grandma, as Gnitle skipped away with Julia to study.

"Dear me," said grandma, talking to herself as she replaced the eatables, "I would put these on and off twenty times rather than not have her eat, for if she should get sick again this Winter, how lonesome the house would be." Thus grandma soliloquized.

Meanwhile the two were studying with all their might, Julia asking a question now and then. At nine o'clock they were ready to recite, which they accomplished without making a blunder.

The next morning Gnitle walked in school, looking fresh and cheerful. No mistakes that day while going through the routine of duty.

Thus the Fall passed pleasantly away. Mr. W—— called occasionally to see the 'olks generally, so this suited Gnitle, and as her mother was too much occupied to see him evenings, his calls were made in the afternoon; Gnitle seldom saw him, as she was usually out walking with Julia and Del.

CHAPTER VII.

"TO-MORROW is the first of December, and my birthday comes three days before Christmas," exclaimed Gnitle.

"The twenty-second of December? The same date as Washington's, had it been in February," said Julia.

"Yes; then I shall be twelve years old, and the next day I can say I'm in my teens," said Gnitle proudly.

For Gnitle, like most little girls, thought the word "teens" sounded large, and to her in particular, those five letters conveyed a hidden charm. Gnitle not only looked forward to this eventful day, but to the holidays as well, for her sister was expected home to spend at least a two weeks' vacation. Julia, too, was looking forward to this bright season, wondering what was in store for her, and wishing St. Nick would deal bountifully.

"I do so hope he'll bring me a muff," said Gnitle, "for my fingers get so cold going to and from school."

Thus these little folks talked while preparing for a good night's rest.

Gnitle and Julia were so busy making presents, they took no note of time as it passed quickly around. Even walks were among the things that were, and lessons, too, were fast becoming so.

"O dear!" exclaimed Gnitle while sewing the fringe on

grandma's shawl, "fingers five I would you drive, and make you do the work of ten: and you ten must work like men, to have this done at ten."

"Well, Gnitle, it seems to me you're in a rhyming mood," said Julia.

"Yes, and in a hurrying one as well, for I have brother's slippers to finish. Mama's and Grace's are now at the shoe store being soled. I cannot rest till they are all done, and I have them carefully hid away, said Gnitle.

Then said Julia, "I mean to give father a handsome hair chain made of mother's hair, and I have mother's slippers nearly finished, so I shan't be behind time with mine."

Thus they worked and talked day after day, feeling as happy as happy could be.

"To-morrow, bright and early, we will see Grace drive up," said Gnitle.

"And me drive away," said Julia, full of glee.

Sure enough, the carriage that brought Grace home took Julia to her's. Thus both made a pleasant exchange, which was to last exactly two weeks. The brother, who was not far away, always spent the Sabbath at home, so the morrow found this happy family together once more.

Family worship and breakfast being over, each one seemed making up their minds where to attend church.

"Now," said grandma, "Mr. Whenford will preach in the church opposite this morning, and I would like to have you all go over to hear him."

"O yes," said Grace, "and brother, let's go. Come, Gnitle, get ready."

"No," answered Gnitle, "I don't care to; his sermon would do me no good."

"Well, then you had better not go, feeling that way," said grandma, "but I would like very much to have you hear him."

"Grandma," said Gnitle, "I would like very much to please you, but I don't feel like hearing him to-day, so please excuse me."

Over went grandma, Grace and her brother, carrying grandma's little foot-stove, while Gnitle and her mother remained at home to prepare dinner.

Little did Gnitle suspect that Mr. W——— would join them at dinner. He being a local preacher, was expected to preach to a Methodist congregation three miles distant, in the afternoon, at half-past three. So grandma, to save him the trouble of driving home, had invited him to dinner.

Gnitle flew around in a lively manner, and when she had finished setting the table, she said "There now, I wish all were here; it will seem so nice to sit down together once more."

She did not wait long, when to her surprise, in came grandma with Mr. Whenford.

After shaking hands with her mother, he extended it to Gnitle, saying "Well, my little girl, I did not see you at church this pleasant morning."

"No," answered Gnitle somewhat coolly, "I did not feel like going."

Then quickly leaving the room, she went in search of grandma.

"Will he be here to dinner"? asked she.

"Yes, child, I invited him over, knowing he would be obliged to preach again this afternoon."

"O dear"! said Gnitle, "I don't grudge him his dinner, but I do wish he would take it somewhere else."

Meanwhile Grace and her brother were extremely polite, entertaining him in the parlor to the best of their ability, little knowing how aggravating his presence was to poor Gnitle.

"O dear"! exclaimed Gnitle as he drove away, "I wish you two would not be so provokingly polite to him again."

"Ah, I know you like him, only you don't like to show it," said Grace, mischievously.

Gnitle's brother knowing she did not relish the joke, said "O let him drive on, we will take a walk to the grave-yard, for it is some time now since I was there."

After walking a half mile, they opened a large gate, then a small one, and ascended a small hill, which in the Summer had been covered with berries; now a slight covering of snow made it appear as white as the tomb-stones peering above its summit. The path being slippery, they were some time ascending.

The top being reached, all remained together, reading the inscriptions on the stones and monuments. When they came to the grave of Mr. Whenford's wife, Grace broke the stillness by saying—

"O, how well I remember her. How many times she has taken tea with mama and grandma, and what a dear, good woman she was to the poor."

"And I wish she were alive now," said Gnitle, "then perhaps we would not be bothered with him."

Grace smiled, and so did her broth[illegible] passed on.

"I begin to feel chilly; this is rather a dreary place to visit; I think I'll not come here again till next Summer," said their brother as they again entered the path.

They soon reached the gates, which they closed carefully, and in a short time were seated by a warm fire.

Supper was soon announced.

"Glad to be alone," said Gnitle, half aloud, "for I did not relish my dinner at all."

After partaking of supper, all went to church except grandma and Grace. While they were seated cozily by the fire, the conversation led grandma to speak of Gnitle's excitement over Mr. Whenford's calling.

"Yes, I notice she does not like to hear anything about him or his family."

"Well, don't tease her," said grandma, "do let her enjoy the holidays all she can, for she has made so much reckoning on them, and your being home. Did you bring the muff"?

"Yes, and I have been waiting a chance to show it to you; so I will go up and get it. I knew she would be rummaging my trunk and room, so I hid it in the garret."

"Never mind getting it; I know if you have selected it, it is a choice and pretty one. So let it be there till Christmas morning."

This was to be grandma's present. Grace had bought her a pretty ring, and her mother's present was to be a maroon velvet bonnet to match her maroon suit, trimmed with maroon velvet. The brother had bought her a fine pair of gloves and a pair of light gaiters, knowing Gnitle's taste in these articles of dress, and he felt quite sure of pleasing her.

Gnitle had kept her presents so carefully concealed, that no one even suspected what they were to receive; all they knew was that she had been very busy.

"Let me see; to-morrow is her birthday, and I mean she shall enjoy it," said grandma. "I have invited Frank and Del to supper. Frank is to bring her a handsome boquet, and Del a locket with her picture in it, and I have a coral necklace laid carefully away. There," said grandma, as she started to get it, "they are coming, so I can't show it now."

Their brother bade them good night, saying "I will be over to dinner to-morrow, for you know I must give Gnitle a dozen love taps to make her remember me."

"Yes, and we'll all make her remember us, won't we grandma"? said Grace, significantly.

"I hope so, but if it was only Summer, so we could get some willow switches, that would be the surest way," added grandma, smiling.

"By the way," added their mother, "Mr. Bonbeaw will will be here to dinner likewise. So I want you all to behave well and look your prettiest. He is a young gentleman of great promise, a lawyer, having the entire charge of the Livingston estate, and will heir a large fortune after the death of his grandfather. His mother and I were young together, and I have always visited the family, but I have not seen any of them since the father's death. Last Tuesday I received a letter from his widow, in which she wrote me her son would be in our vicinity, and if convenient, would dine with us to-morrow. I answered that it would not only be convenient, but that it would afford me the greatest pleasure to have his bright and genial face to cheer us on that memorable day, as that would be Gnitle's birthday, and that all would be home to give him a cordial welcome. So do let us all be up bright and early."

Del's mother sent her over to say that Deaun would be over to help with the dinner, and wait on the table.

"Yes, and she knows how to do it, too," said Gnitle.

The next morning each one was stepping around lively. Even grandma went tripping about, appearing at least ten years younger.

And the way the cookies and pies went in and out of that oven to make room for the big turkey was a caution, or no way slow. Each one was dressed and ready to receive him at half-past eleven.

At twenty minutes of twelve up drove a nobby young gentleman. After giving his colored driver directions concerning the team, he entered, looking and feeling perfectly at home. After shaking hands with the mother and grandma, he extended both hands to Gnitle and Grace. While shaking the hand of Grace he remarked—

"I think this one something more than a child now; I expected to see her the size of this little miss"—pointing to Gnitle. "Why, it does not seem possible that tall and dignified young lady is the little miss I romped with the last time you visited us," said Mr. Bonbeaw, addressing the mother.

"She is the identical Grace that pulled your mustache and chased you from room to room," answered her mother pleasantly. Then, after conversing a few minutes, she said "Now I shall be obliged to leave you with Miss Grace and Gnitle a short time, as my cook has been with me only a short period, and I fear she cannot manage alone."

"Certainly, I am not afraid of her pulling my mustache now," looking roguishly at Grace.

"Well said, as you have none to pull," added Grace.

"We try to look younger as we grow older, you know."

"Yes, but I don't think you'll be troubled with gray hairs or wrinkles for some time to come, judging from your present appearance," said their brother as he entered the room.

"Yes, but care weighs heavily sometimes," answered Mr. Bonbeaw, looking serious.

"Come, Gnitle, are you ready for those taps"?

"O, let me have my dinner first."

"Well, I was commissioned to ask you all out to it, but came near forgetting my errand. So please excuse my remissness, and walk out as quickly as possible."

The order was soon obeyed. Mr. Bonbeaw and Grace were seated on one side of the table, grandma and Gnitle on the other, and mother and son at each end.

"Now, Deaun," said grandma, "you will be obliged to fly around lively," as she dished out the vegetables, "for we are all hungry, and I doubt whether we leave anything behind except the turkey bones and dishes."

Having supplied each one with turkey and vegetables, she gave each a plate of cranberry jelly; then, after handing each a glass of sweet cider, she proceeded to get the dessert in readiness. This consisted of mince pie, fruit-cake, oranges, apples, nuts, and coffee.

"This pie excels any I ever tasted," said Mr. Bonbeaw.

"You'll have another piece to keep me company; bring

me another," said the brother. And away flew Deaun to get one.

"O no, you must excuse me, for with their mother's permission, I intend taking these young ladies for a drive, and what if I could not mount the carriage steps"?

"I'll lend you a helping hand," said the brother.

"And we'll assist, too," added Grace and Gnitle.

"Now, if you ladies will prepare for the drive, I will go over to the hotel and have Sambo here with the team in less than ten minutes. I must be away from here soon after three, as Sambo and I have a long drive before us. It is now two, so we shall have only an hour in which to drive. I have a number of leases to renew, and shall sell thousands of acres before my return, and am expected to dispose of them to the best advantage; so you see I'm not without care. All ready! Here comes Sambo, so let us be off." And away they drove.

Soon after, grandma seated herself, saying "This will be a great day for Gnitle when she returns to find Frank and Del here; it will fill her cup of happiness to overflowing."

Punctually at three all made their appearance, looking as bright as the first rose of Summer. Gnitle was surprised and delighted when she beheld Del and Frank.

"Here is your birthday present," said Frank, handing her the boquet.

"How beautiful and fragrant it is," said Gnitle, smelling it.

"Yes, and are you not going to give me a buttonhole"? asked Mr. Bunbeaw.

"Certainly, and you may take your choice," answered Gnitle, in her charming manner.

After he had selected a red rosebud and geranium leaf, Del stepped forward and placed the locket and chain around her neck, saying, as she did so—

"This is a present from your grandma and your ever true friend Del."

"How beautiful and becoming"! exclaimed Mr. Bunbeaw before Gnitle had recovered from the surprise this present had caused her. Then he added "Well, I can't take any of that with me, so I will be going."

"Will we not see you again"? asked Grace.

"O yes; I shall return through here on New Year's day, and will make a short call."

Then bidding them all good-by, and a "Merry Christmas," he took his departure.

"This has been a most enjoyable day, thus far," said Grace, "but I deeply regret Mr. Bonbeaw being obliged to leave before supper; he is such a lively and agreeable person."

"Yes, missie Grace, and I t'ink he like you bery much, and I t'ink some day he be shinin' up," said Deaun, grinning.

"I can presume he does not think much about the ladies at present, particularly, school girls," answered Grace, changing the subject to address her sister.

"Now, Gnitle, let me see the locket. O what an excellent picture! It is just like life itself."

"That's just why I prize it, and now I must have grandma's in the other side," said Gnitle.

"Now," said Grace, seating herself at the piano, "I feel

just like playing something lively; so choose partners and we'll have a whirl before supper.

All responded, and went skipping and dancing about the room, grandma with them. "For," said she, "birthdays only come once a year."

This amusement being ended, all marched out to supper, feeling they were able to do it ample justice.

"Now, if Mr. Bonbeaw were here, each little lassie would have a laddie," said Deaun, while performing the duties of waitress.

"Yes, Grace looks lonely sitting over there alone," answered the brother.

"I don't feel so," said Grace, "surrounded by so many happy faces. No room for the blues here."

'No, we only make room for the brave," said Frank, "so come and give us that good old song."

All stepped sprightly back to the parlor, and made the old house ring with the "Star Spangled Banner."

"That's too good to be lost; I must join in that too," said grandma, filling up the ring.

The next in order was "Yankee Doodle," "Pop Goes the Weasel," then a polka, and finally a march, which ended in marching some home, and others where they were soon enjoying "tired Nature's sweet restorer, balmy sleep," till long after the sun had risen the next morning, and the village people were astir.

"Come, come," said grandma, waking them all up, "this won't do. Christmas and New Year almost here, mince pies to bake, and the gracious knows what else."

Soon they were all flying around, setting the house in order, and everything being put in its proper place, confusion was fast making room for order, when in popped Mr. Whenford.

"Have called to invite you all to dinner on Christmas, as we are going to have a family gathering."

All seemed delighted with the invitation, except Gnitle. Noticing a look of disappointment, he said—

"There will be a number of boys and girls your size, so you will have a fine time, and I will come with the big sleigh and put all the bells I can on the team of bays; so, you see, I'll be surrounded by 'belles,' and lively ones, too."

This made Gnitle smile, but it did not reconcile her mind in regard to the visit. "For," said she, after he had gone, "I never anticipate any future enjoyment, but he is sure to come and upset all my calculations."

"O we'll have a splendid time," exclaimed grandma. "He has a large and lively family when they are all together. His youngest son is about your age, lively and handsome, the next is a young miss about fourteen, just returned from boarding school, and the other a graduate from the same school about a year ago. She will be company for Miss Grace, and his mother, who occupies a room on the east corner of the house, will be company for me. You should see how straight and sprightly she walks, too. She has her second sight, and so knits and sews while sitting by a bright wood fire, piled high on the andirons, the tops of which she keeps polished so bright you can see your face reflected. Evenings she sits by this bright fire, telling her grandchildren stories by the hour. Now don't be falling in love with her, and forgetting poor grandma."

"No fear," said Gnitle, "don't think I shall fancy any there; don't much think I shall go."

"You will change your mind when Christmas comes," said Grace. Then seeing her mother enter the room, she remarked, "Grandma has been telling us who will entertain each of us."

"I suppose you will be highly entertained by them all—Mr. W——— in particular."

"What shall we wear"? asked Grace in the next breath, fearing she had aroused Gnitle's jealousy.

"O we'll find plenty to wear when Christmas comes; I am in too great a hurry now to discuss the matter," and retired, leaving them to settle the question of dress between them.

Then she entered her room, closed the door carefully and locked it, for she was preparing a surprise for Grace in the shape of a new and elegant silk dress, to be worn on New Year Day. It was a beautiful claret in color, trimmed elegantly with velvet to match. The dress-maker had cut it after her new blue-black silk, and had nearly finished it. So her mother was endeavoring to put on a few finishing touches before laying it away.

"This for New Year and a watch for Christmas, will be two handsome presents, and very useful ones," said her mother, as she laid the dress in a trunk, locking it after her.

Thus the time sped quickly away.

Christmas eve found Grace trying to get Gnitle to bed early.

"For," said she, "you are the baby still, if you are in your teens. So hang up your stocikng; then go to bed and shut your eyes tight, and dream of what Santa Claus will bring you."

"You had better march off too, and keep her company," said her mother, "for grandma and I are well able to look after him. We'll see that he wipes the ashes and soot all off before entering," said the mother, laughingly.

The next morning found each one up bright and early, examining their presents.

"O," said Gnitle, when she saw the muff, "that's just what I've been wishing for." And when she saw the bonnet, gloves, ring and gaiters, said—"Well, grandma, I shan't mind going there to dinner now, for I would not miss wearing all this finery. Just think, a locket and chain, too"!

The next to speak was Grace.

"Didn't I tell you you would change your mind? I did not expect to have a gold watch and chain to wear. I wish it were fashionable to wear embroidered slippers, too, as these are so pretty," exclaimed delighted Grace.

"Now we must go and get our presents, or grandma and mama will think we have forgotten them," said Gnitle.

Off they started, Gnitle bringing her mother's slippers, and a beautiful velvet cloak presented by grandma.

"Well," said her mother, "I'll have something new to wear, too; this is a great surprise."

Then in came Grace with grandma's shawl and an elegant mink cape and muff from her mother.

"Well, well"! said grandma, "I would not miss that sleigh ride—no, no! Not I will be left behind, with this warm cape and muff. So come, let us all get ready."

Just as they were about to do so, in came the brother.

When Gnitle presented him with his slippers and a heavy pair of kids, mounted with fur, he was much pleased, and said—

"These are just what I shall need to make me enjoy the sleigh ride; and the slippers I shall leave here to wear on Sundays, to rest my feet."

Each being fully satisfied with their presents, they proceeded to get ready for the drive. At precisely eleven o'clock up drove a gay span of bays, with bells jingling, buffalo robes shaking, and Mr. W——— smiling when he saw the merry group ready, and waiting to be helped in.

All being seated comfortably, away they drove over a hard, icy crust of snow. They were soon at the house, but as all were seated so nice and comfortably, and the morning being so fine, they concluded to drive four or five miles further; so Mr. W——— sent his little son Hal in to say so, and that they would return in time for dinner. He then gave him an invitation in his off-hand way, peculiar to himself—"Come, Hal, you may jump in, too, as there is a little room." Then taking him between his knees, he drove away at a lively pace.

When they returned, dinner was ready, and so were all to do it justice.

Grandma was shown into his mother's room to warm herself by a blazing wood fire, while the others were ushered to a large room above cozily furnished, and well heated by a wood stove; wood being very plentiful, nothing else was used.

Soon all were seated around a table spread bountifully with turkey, goose, chicken, and everything one could desire. Good appetites were present as well, so you see there was nothing lacking to make this dinner a most enjoyable one, after which the young folks went to sleigh-ride, the eldest son handling the reins.

"Come," said his mother, as they drove away, "seat yourselves by my cozy fire, for I don't enjoy sitting by a stove. It seems to me a dismal way to heat a room; so if you wish me to have anything to say, you must come and sit by my 'stimulator.'"

"Well, mother," said Mr. Whenford, "if that will promote a healthy and vigorous action of the brain, and tongue as well, we will certainly follow."

Accordingly all seated themselves around the old-fashioned fireplace, and held a lively and spirited conversation. When the young people arrived, all assembled in the large parlor, where Miss Grace sang, accompanied with the piano. All were charmed by her melodious voice, and prophesied that she would some day shine as a musical star.

"Hope to be one of the first magnitude, if destiny should thus favor my feeble efforts," answered Grace, smiling, with a look of doubt.

"Now, if you will play a lively march, we'll adjourn to the dining-room and take a social cup of tea to warm us as we journey homeward," said Mr. W———.

"Well, if this is what you call a cup of tea," said grandma, when she beheld the sumptuous table, "then what do you term it when served up plain"?

"We won't wait for music to march us out after this, when Mr. W——— announces tea," remarked some one else.

Then, as Miss Grace walked leisurely in, leaning on the

arm of Sir Walter, she said "I'll take my cup n the shape of fruit-cake and lemonade."

"And mine may take the form of mince pie and coffee," said Grandma. Thus each chose something different, while Gnitle, to be odd and comical, said she would take a pig's-foot.

Down went the servant at Mr. W———'s request, and brought up a large plateful.

"O," said Gnitle, "I did not mean it."

"O, but you must eat one to keep me company," said Mr. W———, making them all laugh.

Thus time passed pleasantly till the. hour arrived for each to say good-night, and again wrap in buffalo robes to be swiftly wafted home by moonlight over glittering snow.

"We're home too soon," said Gnitle when they reached the gate.

Mr. W———, taking the hint, raised the whip and drove on.

"Gnitle, you should not give such broad hints," said grandma, smiling.

"Don't care, so long as people take them."

"Well, I don't believe anybody cares much," said Grace.

"No, for good sleighing never lasts long, so we may as well enjoy it; and I'll come some night this week and take you all out again, for I suppose Miss Grace will return after New Year."

"Yes," answered Grace, "I'm to return the day after. Sorry to leave you all, but I am anxious to proceed with my studies."

"Do not neglect your music," added Mr. W———

"You have a charming voice, and keep perfect time, so I see no reason why you cannot arrive to perfection."

Once more at the gate, Mr. W——— helped them to alight, shook hands all round, and then drove home.

"Well," said Grace, "who can say we did not have a delightful visit."

"Nobody," said Gnitie, "for I never enjoyed a visit more. His mother is just splendid, and so are the children."

"So is Mr. W———," added Grace.

Gnitie made no answer, but went to bed feeling quite different toward him, for the visit had made a good and lasting impression—so much so that when Mr. W——— came to take them for a drive, she was delighted, and on the following Sunday, she went over with Grace and grandma to hear him preach.

CHAPTER VIII.

CHANGES mark the coming years.

We left Gnitle listening attentively to Mr. Whenford's sermon, and as nothing of importance has transpired since, we will say farewell to the Old Year, and pay our compliments to the new, now happily ushered in with clear sky and good sleighing—just what everybody craves on this memorable day. And just what Mr. Bonbeaw was delighted to see

"Now," said he, calling Sambo, "we must be ready to start immediately after breakfast, for I intend taking Miss Grace and Gnitle for a sleigh ride ; I must make them remember me, as I shall not pass through here again—unless something unforeseen should call me—during the next two years."

Thus ended the conversation, and Sambo started to get everything in readiness for the journey.

Breakfast being over, Sambo tapped on the door. "Come, massa, team stanin' at de door, and eberyt'ing ready."

"All right, Sambo, I'll be there in one minute."

In less than five minutes they were wrapped in buffalo robes, and travelling at a lively rate, for the sleigh seemed to propel itself ; and Sambo, several times, instead of giving the team more rein, was obliged to tighten it.

Travelling at such speed, they soon reached their place of destination.

Gnitle had been over to Del's, and was just entering the gate. Mr. Bonbeaw seeing her, alighted and entered the house with her. Grace was seated at the piano, singing a lively air.

Mr. Bonbeaw, wishing to surpise her, slipped quietly behind her, and when she had finished, he clapped his hands, saying " That's very fine, and just what a poor fellow like me needs to cheer and enliven him after more than a two weeks' absence and laborious business the while. And now, Miss Grace, if you will favor me with one more, I will repay you by taking you out sleigh-riding."

" With the greatest of pleasure. What shall it be"? asked Grace.

" ' Should Old Acquaintance Be Forgot ' will please me most."

" And won't you please join in"? asked Grace.

" Yes, and won't you all"? asked Mr. Bonbeaw.

Soon all were participants till the end ; then, as Miss Grace arose, Mr. Bonbeaw extended his hand, saying " Let us shake hands over it," implying a silent promise not to forget each other.

" Now, if you and Gnitle will get ready, we'll be off in as short time as possible."

" We shall expect you to dine with us, Mr. Bonbeaw," said the mother, as her daughters entered prepared for the drive.

" Shall be most happy to, if it will not give you too much trouble," answered Mr. Bonbeaw, as he arose to escort them to the sleigh.

"No trouble whatever, but a pleasure," answered the mother.

"I shall return then, and make you twice glad," said Mr. Bonbeaw, as they drove away.

When they passed Mr. Whenford's, Grace told him how pleasantly they had spent Christmas Day.

"O," said Mr. Bonbeaw, "you must all have had a splendid time; wish I could have been there. Think I'll be obliged to keep my eye on Sir Walter and the widower," he added, jokingly. "And how about Hal, Gnitle"?

"Ah, he's a bright little fellow, and handsome, too; that's the most I can say of him," answered Gnitle.

"Think that's complimentary enough," said Mr. Bonbeaw, smiling. "Hope you both may always enjoy Christmas and New Year Day, for of all days in the year, these should be the happiest. And now, if you think we have driven far enough, I'll turn back, so we will not keep them waiting dinner."

The three kept up a lively conversation till they reached home; then handing the reins to Sambo, all entered the house, looking rosy, mischievous, and quite hungry. After showing Mr. Bonbeaw where he could arrange his toilet, the two went to dress for dinner.

When Miss Grace entered the dressing-room, there was the elegant silk dress, on which was pinned a small slip of paper, which read as follows:

"This is a Christmas present reserved for you to wear to-day, so please appear in it, to oblige MAMA."

Grace was not long obeying the order, and soon joined them below, looking delighted, and it is needless to say, charming.

"Now," said her mother, "just play a march, and by the time you are through dinner will be ready."

"O yes, that will be a nice way to make us forget hunger," added Mr. Bonbeaw.

"I'm afraid it will have a contrary effect, and sharpen my appetite," answered Grace, seating herself at the piano.

When she had finished playing, all went to dinner, feeling they could dispatch turkey, chicken, mince pie, and a dozen more things equally good, in the shortest space of time.

"Think there will be no need of an appetite restorer till we are through," said Mr. Bonbeaw, when seated.

"I'll reserve mine till the next meal," said Grace, significantly.

"Better keep it till to-morrow, said Gnitle, meaningly, as that was the day set for Grace to return.

Dinner being over, all passed into the parlor and held a spirited conversation till the time arrived for Mr. Bonbeaw to think of leaving.

"I suppose when Miss Grace and I shall take leave of you all, everything will go on again in the even tenor," said Mr. Bonbeaw, addressing the mother.

"Yes, but I shall not open school till Monday to-morrow being Friday."

"Will the little teacher be on duty, too"? asked he, addressing Gnitle.

"O yes, I'm always ready to teach and be taught," answered Gnitle, in her pleasant tone.

"Good for you," added Mr. Bonbeaw, "that's what I like to hear. And are you ready for the latter"? asked he, looking mischievously at Grace.

"O yes," said Grace, "I am ready and only too anxious to get through before the expiration of another year."

"Hope you may, and that you will graduate with distinction," answered Mr. Bonbeaw.

"That has been and shall be my aim," said Grace, "and unless something unforeseen occurs to hinder, think I shall accomplish it."

"I have no doubt but you will sound the trumpet of excelsior, and receive the scroll given to the industrious and deserving, before we meet again, which, if nothing prevents, will be in a couple of years. And as I have your mother's permission, I'll now present you with a small keepsake."

Then placing a heavy chased ring—with a hand carved exquisitely, holding a large pearl between its forefinger and thumb—on the forefinger of her right hand, said—

"I place it here that it may be conspicuous, and better serve as a reminder. Let the pearl represent Education and Religion, the two pearls of priceless worth. And when I return, I hope to find you have graduated with all the honors, and if you have not embraced the other, shall know you are on the stepping-stone leading to it."

Then cordially shaking her hand, he turned to say a few words to Gnitle.

"And you, my little friend, will have taken Grace's place by that time, and I shall expect to meet another tall and dignified young lady."

"No doubt, at least I hope so," said Gnitle, with a pleased look.

Then bidding grandma and the mother good-by, he left, promising to write them inside of a week.

"That young fellow will make friends wherever he goes; he is manly and genial ; his face is not only intellectual, but carries sunshine with it. What a bright and cheering beam he must be to his mother, when we, comparatively strangers, already adore him. Dear me ! How lonely I felt to see him drive away," said grandma.

Could you have seen the other faces, you would have concluded grandma was not the only one that felt grieved to see him depart, for all looked lonely, though they did not express themselves as fervently as grandma.

In an hour or two after, up drove Mr. Whenford and Sir Walter.

"I have come to make a New Year call," said Mr. W——, "and Walter, knowing Miss Grace expects to leave on the morrow, has come to take the young ladies out sleigh-riding."

"Nothing could please me better," said Grace, rising.

"And me," said Gnitle.

Then away they hurried to put on thicker clothing, for it had grown very chilly since five o'clock. When they made their appearance, each with a muff, hood, and warm cloak, Sir Walter exclaimed—

"I see you mean to bid defiance to Jack Frost," as he helped them in and tucked the robes in around them.

While the young people were enjoying the ride, Mr. Whenford was regaling himself with turkey, mince pie, and coffee. When he had finished, he looked quite serious, and said—

"This day must settle the question whether I'm to remain a widower. Can't endure suspense any longer ; so now it remains with you to make me happy or miserable."

"By saying 'yes,' I may render you more than miserable," said the widow, smiling.

"Well, one can't be miserable alone, so I shall have company," anwered Mr. W———. "I suppose I may take it for granted we are to share it together? Silence gives consent. Now I will ask grandma. Well, grandma, what say you in regard to the matter? And when will it be convenient for you to have her leave you"?

"As regards the first, she is old enough to answer for herself. To the latter I can answer that it will not be convenient for me to part with her till Spring. Then her sister, who is now travelling with her husband, will return, and be glad to occupy part of the house, as she writes me they are tired of boarding. I shall reserve this large room, and a sleeping room for Gnitle and myself. Julia can remain with us till Grace has finished her education, and by that time Gnitle will be prepared to take her place. Thus Gnitle and Julia will be company for me and each other; studying their lessons together is a help to both. It quite amuses me when they ask each other questions."

"Not only that," answered Mr. W———, "but it brings back old associations and things almost forgotten."

"Yes, and perhaps that is why I am amused and delighted when they sit down to study. I hope they may remain together as helpmates till their school days are over. I shall be very sorry to lose their company, but perhaps I may be called to leave them, and not they me; so I shall not worry about the future. Whichever way, I trust it will be bright for all."

"Then I suppose you will all board with your daughter"?

"Yes, this will be her home while I live, be it long or short, and Gnitle's, too."

"What time, or in which month, will your daughter arrive"?

"The last of March, or the first of April; but it will cause us to be somewhat unsettled for at least two weeks, so I think there had better be no change made here till the last of the month."

"It shall be as you desire," answered Mr. W———, feeling much relieved.

In this matter-of-fact way the question was settled before the young people drove up. Not much romance connected with it. No, not much, but rather a comical and off-hand manner of settling such an important question. Well, as "all's well that ends well," it matters little which presides.

"Come," said Grace, "drive the horses under the shed, for you have given us a great treat, and now it is my turn."

"Agreed," said Sir Walter; "I never refuse a treat, particularly on New Year Day. I shall obey your order, and join you in a few moments."

Only a few moments elapsed before all were seated around the table. Grandma had everything in readiness, knowing how good a warm supper tastes after a cold Winter night's drive.

"And now we'll have our cup of tea," said grandma, as they (the older ones) seated themselves around a smaller table in the sitting-room.

Mr. W———, peeping in the dining-room, said "Well, if sleigh riding makes these young ladies so rosy and lively, Sir Walter may come to-morrow and drive Miss Grace back, and that will give Gnitle a chance to accompany her, and Julia can return likewise. Unless we get an early start, Julia will have gone before we meet her, for I was to return with their conveyance."

"Say we make it half-past nine," said Sir Walter.

"That's the time I was going to suggest, as they will not start till after dinner," answered Grace.

"Very well, I shall be here punctually at the time mentioned."

Then said Mr. W———, "I had no idea it was so late, so if you have decided when to start, we'll be going, and give the young ladies a few hours rest before morning."

They then departed, wishing them happy dreams, and that the sun would shine brightly on the morrow. And I presume that their future will be ever bright and unclouded.

Said Grace, as they were retiring for the night—"If we go through the year as pleasantly as we have commenced, we shall certainly pass a happy one. There's one thing certain, we have had plenty of sleigh rides. To morrow, another."

"Ten miles each way will make twenty for me," said Gnitle; "how I shall enjoy it! I'll have your company going down, and Julia's coming back, so I shall have a lively time."

Talking thus, they fell asleep, and awoke to find the sun shining brightly, and the weather a few degrees warmer.

"Come, breakfast is ready," said grandma.

"So are we," answered Gnitle. "Yes, sleigh-rides make people fly around lively."

"Well, it is best to hurry matters ; so come, as Grace has her trunk to pack."

Breakfast being over, the trunk was soon in readiness, and the young ladies, too. So all sat down together to await Sir Walter's arrival, the mother advising Grace in relation to her studies, as all good mothers and fathers do who are anxious to promote their children's welfare.

The time having arrived, Sir Walter appeared, driving briskly.

"Well, I see you have brought fine weather with you," exclaimed their mother.

"Yes, nothing like sunshine and lively 'belles'; they will keep a fellow's heart light if anything will," said Sir Walter, assisting them in.

"You are not going to leave the trunk behind," said grandma.

"O no ; trunks always go with 'belles.'" Then placing it under the seat, he drove away, all waiving their hands to the dear ones left behind.

The road being all the way descending, enabled them to travel the ten miles in just an hour. Half-past ten found them at Julia's residence.

She and her father had just returned from a sleigh-ride. The young people were delighted to meet, while the father seemed greatly pleased as he shook hands all around. Then inviting Sir Walter to remain and have dinner with them, he sent his colored driver out to take charge of the team. All then entered the house together, where they were met by Julia's mother.

"Well, well, you have the start of Julia and her father."

"Yes," said Sir Walter, "I meant Gnitle to have a sleigh ride, too."

"Very kind and thoughtful of you."

"I shall be obliged to give father the credit, for it was his suggestion, also to have Julia accompany us back."

"Yes, I see; it will make it very pleasant for both. Now you must all be hungry, so please walk out to dinner."

Julia's father being very social, and all feeling the influence of the new year, joined in a spirited conversation. After dinner all went for a drive. Julia having her trunk in readiness, there was nothing to do but to place it under the seat where Grace's had lodged so recently.

At three all bade each other good-by, feeling very happy. Julia and Grace once more exchanging homes.

"I have the best of Grace," said Julia, as they drove away, "for I have you for company, while she has no one but mama and papa. We have splendid times, don't we, Gnitle"?

"Yes, when you don't tease me over your lessons," answered Gnitle, mischievously. "How about Christmas"? she then asked.

"O, mama and papa were delighted with what I gave them, and I received just what I was wishing for."

Thus they chatted, Sir Walter joining them whenever it was opportune, till they reached home.

"Here we are," said he, helping them alight. "We have been just an hour and a half returning."

"That was pretty rapid speed, considering it was all uphill work. Won't you come in and have supper with us before you drive home"? asked grandma.

" No, thank you, I have an engagement for this evening, so shall be obliged to leave immediately." Then saying "good-by till we meet again," he drove away.

" Well, I'm pleased to see you little folks back again ; now everything is ready, so let us have supper," said grandma.

" Where is mama " ?

" O she went to make a few calls, and has not returned yet. You know when people get talking over Chirstmas and New Year, they .never know when to stop," said grandma in her quaint style, and I'll add, old-fashioned, too.

It was not long before the mother entered. After kissing each, she asked Julia how she had enjoyed the holidays, and what her presents were.

" Here they are," said Julia, showing a tiny watch and chain with a small locket attached. " They are what I told Gnitlė would please me."

" I am delighted to see you were not disappointed. And here is a pretty book you may keep to remember me. The gift is small, but it will serve as a reminder of days past and gone. To-morrow you and Gnitle must go over to see Del, for she sent particular word to both. Then you can all call on the doctor's wife, as she wished to be remembered, and is very anxious to see Gnitle.

The next morning being Saturday, both began to get out •their books, thus making preparation for Monday. Both loved school, and were delighted to think the time was drawing near. In the afternoon both went over to see Del, where they were treated to every kind of delicacy, and wished many long and happy years.

The three then proceeded to make the other call.

"Happy New Year"! exclaimed Frank and his mother in the same breath, as they entered.

"Thank you," said each, extending their hand, "and may you both live to enjoy many."

"Well, Gnitle," said the doctor's wife, "you have not kept your promise; you said you would come to see me often."

"I know, but I was so very busy preparing for Christmas. So please excuse me, and I'll commence now and do better. How is the doctor"?

"Well and jolly as ever," said his wife.

"Please wish him a happy new year for me," said Gnitle.

"And for us all," added the rest.

"I will do so with pleasure."

Frank then brought in cake and pie of every description. Then he said "I have lemonade, wine, and coffee —which shall it be"?

"Lemonade," answered each.

"I don't see why the ladies generally prefer lemonade, unless it is because they are often sour, and need sweetening," said Frank.

"You are very sharp; I think you have been taking some without sugar," added Gnitle.

After partaking of this beverage, Frank asked them to take a little wine.

"I can whine enough without it," said Gnitle, jokingly.

"There's the effect of the lemonade, it must have been too sour," said Frank, mischievously.

"The two jokers are together again," said the doctor's wife, smiling.

"You must have had a lively time last Summer," said Julia.

"Yes, and I often wish I could have them over again. Not that I wish Gnitle to get sick; oh, no! But I wish she were with us again."

"We could not spare Gnitle," said Julia. "I would be travelling home again in less than a week if I were deprived of her cheerful face and lively company."

"And I find it very nice to have her so near me again," said Del. "Well, I wish she was a little nearer me, that I could see her often."

"O I'll come to see you now, and make you and Frank twice glad," said Gnitle, as they arose to depart.

"No danger, you can't do it," said Frank. "Too great a feat for a little body like you to perform."

"Yes," answered the doctor's wife, "you'll never be able to make us more than *once* glad, and that will be when you call on us. Shall be happy to see these young friends with you whenever they have leisure."

After extending an invitation to mother and son to call, they took their departure, feeling they had had a most enjoyable visit, or call, as we term it.

All retired early feeling somewhat fatigued, for the two weeks had been quite exciting. Mind and body required rest. The day appointed by an all-wise God was fast approaching, and was always kept sacred by this little family. The brother was always at home on that all-important day. In the morning Gnitle placed his slippers near the fireplace, knowing he would enjoy wearing them. She took great delight in pleasing him and making his home attractive.

In the evening, grandma, Julia, Gnitle, and the brother went over to hear Mr. Whenford preach.

"He must have an excellent memory not to require notes," said Julia, when they were walking home.

"Yes, he very often opens his Bible, picks out his text, and prepares his sermon in a couple of [illegible] known him to do it in less time. They are [illegible] family," said grandma.

"Yes," added the brother, "and a very happy one, to all appearance. From what Gnitle tells me you must have had a delightful time on Christmas Day."

"I almost wish I had been with you," said Julia.

The brother entered, but did not tarry long. [illegible] he bade them good night, saying "To-morrow you [illegible] travelling off to school."

"Yes," said grandma, "best place for them."

"So we think," replied Julia.

"Yes, and I shall be ready to make them all stand around again," said Gnitle, significantly.

The next morning over came Del with her pile of books.

"This looks like business again," said the mother as they all prepared to leave.

Said grandma—"Don't be talking your throats sore the first day."

"We'll guard against that," said Gnitle.

The children were all there, looking bright and fresh, and all seemed delighted to behold the little teacher. Several of the scholars gave her some pretty and useful presents.

Thus the first school hours of the new year passed pleasantly away. Julia, Del, and Gnitle took their accustomed walk before studying their lessons.

While they were gone, Gnitle's mother said—"I shall not tell Gnitle yet what decision I have arrived at, lest it make her nervous, and likewise unfit her for school duties."

Then said grandma—"As you will probably resign your situation to Mr. Van and wife the last of February, I would not tell her till then. I don't think she will feel as badly now, but still it might have a disheartening tendency, so better let well enough alone. I don't wish to be obliged to give her another pill," said grandma, laughing.

The latter part of the week brought a letter from Mr. Bonbeaw, in which he wrote as follows :

"Grandfather Bonbeaw has written for mother and myself to come to him as soon as possible, as his health is in a very precarious condition. Accordingly, nothing preventing, we will sail the first of February. Mother sends much love to you all, and requests me to say that she dreads the journey. Will write you again when we reach Paris.

With much love to you all, I am your very true friend, BONBEAW."

The mother then wrote Grace, giving her this news, and likewise telling or writing of the change she was contemplating.

Grace felt sorry to know Mr. Bonbeaw was going so far away, but was pleased with the idea of having Mr. W—— for a stepfather. She reasoned somewhat as grandma had with Gnitle the Sunday evening Mr. W—— called. Grace had been told all in relation to that eventful night. In a few days she answered her mother's letter, in which she wrote :

"I am sorry to hear that Mr. Bonbeaw and mother are going so far away ; but I am not sorry in regard to the latter. Think you have come to a wise conclusion, and believe you will never have cause to regret it Don't tell Gnitle till you are through teaching.

With much love to all, I am your affectionate daughter, GRACE."

CHAPTER IX.

DURING the intervening time nothing of importance occurred, so we will now dwell a few moments on the last day of February.

Mr. Van having arranged to proceed with the school on the first of March, all things were duly and agreeably settled. In the morning Gnitle's mother called both pupils, and said—

"Well, Gnitle, I told you, or rather promised, when I contemplated making a change I would tell you. This will be the last day you will assist mama in teaching, as I have resigned my situation to Mr. Van and wife. The last of April I expect to change my name for that of Mrs. Whenford."

Gnitle looked surprised, and simply said "Well, mama, you know best." Then, with tears in her eyes, she walked out to grandma, saying "Well, it seems we are doomed to meet with a change after all. I did so hope——" and there she stopped, too full to say more.

"Never mind, child, it is all for the best. Your aunt will come and take charge here, and you, Julia, and I will have fine times together. Besides, you will have more time to study and less work."

"Very true, but I love to teach," answered Gnitle.

"Come," said the mother, "we must be off. This will

be a holiday. There will be but little teaching done, as I shall dismiss at twelve."

So off they started, Gnitle feeling somewhat sad over the change, but grandma's words had cheered her and made her heart less heavy.

When they reached the school, Del, who was sure to notice any change in Gnitle's appearance, was standing in the doorway.

"You don't look well, Gnitle," said Del.

"I feel pretty well, but a little nervous."

"Over what"?

"You'll know soon enough," answered Gnitle, in a low tone.

Just then all were requested to take their accustomed places.

School being opened, the mother talked to the children a short time, and finally announced to them that she was about to leave, and that the school would be opened the first of March by Mr. Van Switt and wife.

The children were all in tears, and assembled around Gnitle, saying—

"And are we to lose our little teacher, too"?

"Yes," answered Gnitle, "as a teacher, but I shall remain with you a scholar once more."

"Then we will see you every day, but we would like you to teach us," said several voices.

"And so do I," answered the little teacher affectionately.

After writing a short time, the children were given a long recess, and then were called in and dismissed. Each took their parting kiss, as a mother, of course, before going, and how those little tongues spread the news around while travelling home. And when they reached there with the news, their mothers were all too much surprised to believe it. Several put on their bonnets and shawls, and ran over to the widow's to see whether they had been informed correctly, and when told such was true, expressed much sorrow over the unexpected change.

Having informed you how Gnitle, scholars, and parents received the news, we will pass from the last of February to the first of March.

The school was then opened, Mr. and Mrs. Van Swift presiding. Both being very efficient teachers, general satisfaction was the result. Gnitle and Julia soon became greatly attached to Mrs. Van, while she in turn considered them two of her brightest pupils.

Now I think in relation to the school I have written all that will interest you, so let us turn our attention to other matters, perhaps of less importance, for to me it seems there is nothing of so much value to the young as a school presided over by competent and patient teachers. Of course I know no teacher is competeut unless patient, but I fear there are many who lack this virtue. Too many think education is all there is required to make them successful teachers. To patiently explain the lessons is another requisite. When able to do this, success is sure to follow, and no one can detect this quality in a teacher as soon as a child. I know you will thauk me for this compliment, and wish me to enlarge and give them a few graceful hints. Enough has been administered, as I believe in small doses, so we will go back to the little teacher, her mother, and the rest of the folks in general.

Mr. Whenford's visits became more frequent. The

mother feeling her time not so much occupied, received him occasionally, evenings.

Gnitle seemed perfectly reconciled to the change, or at least had come to the same conclusion she had arrived at from the first—"That there would be no use contending."

On April first her aunt and uncle arrived, and took possession of part of the house. All boarding with them till the all-important event took place on the last of April.

Mr. Whenford being a Methodist, and the widow a Baptist, it was arranged that Julia's parents, Grace, and the Baptist minister should drive up in the early part of the evening, and at nine o'clock the ceremony would take place. His family were all to be present, and a few of the widow's very intimate friends.

Grandma and the aunt had arranged for a grand supper at ten o'clock, thus giving those who had a long distance to drive ample time to reach home before twelve.

The bride was attired in steel colored silk, trimmed heavily with velvet and fringe. The groom wore a plain black broadcloth suit, a black tie, and pearl colored kids. Grace wore the claret silk which was presented to her on New Year day. Gnitle a pink silk, and Julia a blue one. His youngest daughter wore a muslin trimmed with very fine and elegant needle-work, while the other was dressed in a rick blue silk, made in the tip of the fashion. His mother wore a lovely quaker colored silk, and quaker cap. Grandma was dressed in a heavy black satin, and wore a lovely cap her daughter had brought from abroad. The aunt wore a crimson corded silk, which was very becom-ing, she being a brunette.

Sir Walter and Hal looked charming, as a matter of

course. And so did every one present not only look charming, but happy and satisfied.

His family were all delighted, and anxious to see the marriage consummated.

A few minutes after nine o'clock they were joined in wedlock, and at ten the usual ceremony of wishing joy and shaking hands was over, and all had marched out to supper.

Miss Grace presiding as usual at the piano, Sir Walter remained to escort her to the dining-room.

Thus sped the time; every one being truly happy.

After supper the young people assembled in the parlor, Miss Grace again seated at the piano playing for those who chose to dance, while the others retired to the sitting-room to hold a spirited conversation, wit and humor presiding.

At eleven o'clock, Julia's father and mother, the minister and Grace, took their departure. Grace would have tarried with them longer, had she not felt it her duty to attend school the following day, so she returned with them, for she knew that unless she improved every moment she would miss her aim, and not receive the scroll awarded to the industrious and persevering.

The rest were not long following their example.

Sir Walter drove Mr. W——, wife, and grandmother home first, then returned for his sisters and Hal.

At twelve all were driving rapidly toward home, while those already there were eating or dreaming over wedding-cake; and had you been there, I know you, like myself, would have preferred eating it. Could you have seen the big bundles of cake Del, Julia, and Gnitle put under their pillows, you would have made up your mind that some people believe in dreams.

"Well," said grandma, "weddings don't take place every day, and thankful am I they do not, for I am completely worn out."

"Well," answered Gnitle, trying to be consoling, "things will go on again in the even tenor."

"I hope so, for I believe there are more people killed by undue excitement, than die from natural causes."

"Yes," said Gnitle, "excitement is very injurious, especially when one is obliged to fall back on an opium pill."

This speech caused all to laugh heartily, for grandma never thought of it without smiling.

Then said Julia, "If I had to attend many weddings or parties, I should not care to study many lessons, for indeed I, too, am tired"!

"Just take a little of 'Mrs. Winslow's Soothing Syrup,' and retire," answered Gnitle.

"That's just the remedy you should have resorted to the Sunday evening you took the pill," said Julia, laughingly.

"O no, that would not have been powerful enough," said Gnitle, seriously, making them all laugh again.

"Come, come, you'll never learn your lessons at this rate," exclaimed grandma; then she remarked rather mischievously, "Mr. W—— and his bride will probably drive down to see us."

"Yes," answered Gnitle, "mama said she would come nearly every day to see us, and when the days get warmer she would send for us every Saturday."

"I shall go too," said grandma."

" Certainly, you will go, for I would not to go without you — no, not for the world. We are to remain together, for that was the promise the night you administered the pill."

" Do you want to make me laugh again " ?

" Yes, grandma, for I would like to see you grow fat."

" O don't wish such a calamity as that upon me, the Summer coming, too. Mr. Whenford's team likewise might suffer from the effects of such a heavy load."

In the afternoon, up drove Mr. and Mrs. W———, who had come to make a short call, and to invite them all there on Saturday.

" Well, grandma," said Mr. W———, " I suppose you are glad the wedding is over " ?

" Yes, I am, for a quiet life suits me best, and if you live long enough you'll think so, too."

" Well, grandma, when you come Saturday we will have a quiet time all to ourselves. I'm going to—well, I won't tell you now, only that I'll make you a splendid old-fashioned cup of tea besides."

" All right, I understsnd what that means. What time will you be here " ?

" Immediately after breakfast, so all be in readiness," said Mr. W——.

Meanwhile Mrs. W——— conversed with Gnitle and Julia, asking them questions in relation to school, hoping at the same time they would be able to graduate, and return together by the time Grace was through.

Mr. W——— said, as they drove away, " All be ready when I come." And all were ready and waiting. It is needless for me to say all had a delightful time, for who cannot have with plenty of agreeable company and everything good to eat?

In the evening all returned home, wishing Saturday came twice a week instead of once. This programme was kept up all the Summer, occasionally Del and Frank accompanying them.

The brother now having two homes to visit, took dinner with his mother, and supper with grandma and Gnitle. Having had an excellent offer from a firm on Broadway, New York city, he concluded to accept it. Then bidding the loved ones good-by, he left to seek his fortune. All missed him very much when Sunday came, but were pleased to see him ambitious, and anxious to see something of the world.

The weather had grown quite cool, consequently their Saturday pleasure trips became less frequent, as grandma's asthma would not be improved by cold and exposure to the night air. Knowing this, Mr. and Mrs. W——— came every Saturday afternoon to make a short call, bringing them nuts, apples, cakes, and nice fresh milk for grandma, hoping it would strengthen her. The aunt and uncle had grown very fond of Gnitle, and thought just as everybody else, that she was a little treasure.

During the latter part of the Fall, the uncle fell from a chestnut tree and broke his arm. Gnitle tried hard to make him forget his pain and loneliness by reading to him whenever she was at leisure. Grandma, too, was also very attentive while her daughter was engaged with the household duties. But poor grandma's health was fast failing, and she said each day her time here would be short.

One day, while grandma and Gnitle were sitting alone, grandma seemed unusually lively and talkative.

"I suppose, Gnitle, you will be all through your studies and ready to leave me in the Spring, but I often feel I shall not remain with you till then ; so I will tell you now what I would like you to do in the future. You have an imaginative mind, which you can greatly improve by travelling, and if you ever have the means at your command, promise me you will do so. Do try and see as much of the world and the people in it as possible. Now, you'll remember what grandma says, won't you" ?

"O yes, grandma, nothing could please me better ; but you know people cannot travel without means."

"Very true, but the proviso was, if ever you have the means to do so."

Just then Julia came in to study her lessons, and thus the conversation ended. This was the latter part of November, and on the twenty-second of Decemher—Gnitle's birthday—grandma breathed her last.

Her two children and Gnitle could not realize it at first.

"O what changes in one short year," said the aunt.

"Yes, and a year to-day grandma was enjoying the day with us. O how I shall prize the locket and chain ! I am so delighted to think I have her picture in it," added Gnitle, kissing it. "I little thought then that I should prize the gift more on my coming birthday than then."

The day before Christmas, a large assemblage paid their last honors to the dead. Then slowly proceeded the procession till they reached the large gate opening into the graveyard ; then on up the hill, the bell tolling slowly till they had reached the top, and grandma carefully consigned to mother earth.

"O," said Gnitle, as they drove home, "how I shall miss her. It will not seem like home to me any more."

"Nor to me," said Julia, "but we will try to be as happy together as possible. Your aunt and uncle think the world of you, and will try to take grandma's place."

"That can never be done. No mortal living can take her place here," putting her hand on her heart.

It is needless for me to say more, as I have already penned the poem written by Gnitle after her grandma's death, which expresses how fervent and deep-seated Gnitle's affections were.

The holidays were spent pleasantly, but how quiet and subdued all appeared—how different from the previous year.

The uncle and aunt, Gnitle and Julia, spent New Year day at Mr. Whenford's. When they left, the mother promised to come nearly every day to see them, and Mr. W—— said he would take Mrs. W——, Gnitle and Julia to see Grace some fine Saturday, and would come for them early on Monday morning, and return in time for school.

"O that will be splendid," said Julia and Gnitle, "we can all go to church, and it will give us quite a visit."

The weather being stormy several Saturdays in succession, the contemplated visit was postponed some five or six weeks.

Meanwhile, grandma's will was opened, which was as follows:

"To my daughter Julia, the house opposite and lot joining the garden on the southeast corner.

"To my granddaughter Gnitle, the $15,000 deposited by me in the

Ulster Bank when she arrives at the age of eighteen, to hold and do with as her judgment shall then dictate.

"To this my last will and testament I do this day affix my name and seal, in the presence of these witnesses: CATHERINE E. DUSHAY.

"JOHN JONES.

"SAMUEL SMITH."

I will not say that the document was in just this shape, or drawn up verbatim, but that was its purport. As I have not made law a study, I will ask you to be lenient in regard to its preciseness, and take the will for the deed.

When Gnitle had heard the contents of the will, it flashed upon her mind what grandma meant when she said "the proviso is, if you ever have the means." "Now I see plainly what grandma was thinking of, and if the Lord spares me, I shall do as she desired."

No one except Gnitle seemed surprised at the manner grandma had disposed of her property. For all knew that Gnitle was dearer to grandma than any one living. Perhaps one reason was, they had always shared each other's joys and sorrows.

"I think to-morrow will be a pleasant day, so we will drive down and tell them to be ready bright and early." And the weather was just as Mr. Whenford had predicted.

Some snow had fallen during the night; this with the hard crust already formed, made the sleigh glide along swiftly. Having started at nine, at ten they were at Julia's home.

After helping them out, Mr. W——— stopped long enough to say "how do you do," and "good-by," and then hurried home to transact some important business.

Julia's parents and Grace were delighted to find they could remain until Monday. After dinner the young people retired to Grace's room, it being cozy and quiet. When seated, Grace spoke of the changes there had been in their family circle, and all within eight months; then recounted each as they had occurred—"Mama married, brother in the city, grandma dead—no, not dead, only sleeping", said Grace thoughtfully.

"Do you hear from brother often"?

"Yes, and he writes that he is well satisfied with his employers, and is quite sure they are with him."

"Has mama heard from Mr. Bonbeaw recently"?

"He wrote only a few days ago that his grandfather had died since he wrote me last, and left him the whole of his vast estate. He likewise wrote that Mr. Livingston had written him he would require his services the first of September, as he would then sell a large portion of the estate."

"Then he will pass through here before the two years shall have expired," said Grace. "He promised to call on us."

"Yes, and he has not forgotten his promise, for he wrote mama—'I am very anxious to see you all, but,' he added, 'mother's health is very poor, so I shall be obliged to return almost immediately. And when I am through disposing of the land, and everything is in lawful shape, so there will be no need of my presence again, shall surrender my charge to some one else.'"

"Then," answered Grace, looking at the ring, "I am sure I shall graduate this Spring, and with honor, too; and to-morrow shall embrace the other pearl, so I shall have accomplished and embraced all he wished this pearl to represent before he arrives."

" How very kind of him to take such an interest in your welfare," remarked Julia. " Am sorry I did not have the pleasure of seeing him, for from what Gnitle has told me, I judge him to be quite uncommon."

Just then the bell rang, and all went down to supper.

" Well, mama," said Grace, " your coming to-day was a great surprise, and a very pleasant one."

" Well, child, you would have seen us long before this, had the weather proved favorable."

"That of course would have pleased me, but I am better pleased that you are all here now."

" So are we ; I will answer for all being informed of the morrow."

" And no doubt we shall return home fully satisfied and happy, after witnessing the pleasant surprise you have in store for us on the morrow."

" Yes, mama, and I, too, shall feel better satisfied when I have done what I consider to be a duty I owe my Saviour. I wish to acknowledge Him in all my ways, and unless I proclaim my love and gratitude to the world, I need not expect His blessings."

" Very true, my daughter ; if we accept Him here, He will, according to His promise, accept us in that beautiful world beyond."

Here the conversation ended, and all went for a walk, after which the mother conversed with Grace alone for a short time in regard to the step she was about to take. She then retired, feeling fully convinced her child was truly converted, and felt the importance of the step she so soon would take.

Sunday was an unusually bright day, and the church was

crowded with eager spectators. There were several young converts beside Grace, and each having a large circle of friends, made it a very interesting occasion. Then followed an eloquent sermon and fine singing, making it a most enjoyable season for all. After partaking of the Sacrament, their names were enrolled for service in the cause of Christ. The gifted preacher then asked—"Who would not enlist under such a Leader, and work faithfully 'neath the banner, 'Christ, our Saviour'"?

The next morning Mr. Wheaford drove up at half-past seven; he remained just long enough to congratulate Grace on the choice she had made so recently. "For," said he, "you will find you have never known what true happiness was before, and each hour, day and year you'll realize it more and more." Then, bidding all good-by, he drove back in time for school.

And now, as their time was principally devoted to school, going to church, and writing to absent ones, calling on Del and the doctor's wife occasionally, and frequently visiting Mr. Whenford's, we will remark on what took place the first of May:

One change follows another. Del's father sold out his business to the overseer of the factory, and bought a beautiful dwelling opposite the academy that Julia and Gnitle were now attending, they having entered a few weeks previous; so they saw each other frequently, although they did not attend the same school. Del and Nenie were attending the seminary in which their oldest sister had been a pupil for a number of years.

In a few days Frank called to bid them all good-by. Finding them all together enjoying a pleasant afternoon at Del's, he concluded to remain with them an hour, as that would just give him time to reach the boat in season.

"Well," said he, "you young ladies thought to leave me behind, but you see I've caught up with you, and shall soon pass you on the way."

"Why, where are you expecting to land"? asked each of them in the same breath. "Not where Christopher Columbus did, are you"?

"No, nor where Robinson Crusoe did, either; but I'm going to the city of New York to study with a noted physician and surgeon, who is an old friend of father's."

"O, I see," said Gnitle, "your father is well aware he'll make you mind your P's and Q's, and that's why he sends you, and when I break my neck you'll be the first surgeon I shall call on."

As the time approached for him to leave, all grew more serious; common sense taking the place of nonsense.

"Well," said Gnitle, as he extended his hand to say good-by, "I suppose you will see brother frequently."

"Yes, and shall endeavor to room with him, if I find he has no one, and will be so compassionate and accommodating."

"Why do you say compassionate? Do you expect to grieve so you'll need sympathy? asked Gnitle.

"I shall be lonesome among entire stranger."

"O you'll soon get used to new faces, and probably will be attracted to them, and strange sounds and sights will soon cease to attract."

"Quite a sermon. Think I'd better be going."

Then looking at the time, he found he had just time to

reach the boat. Then shaking hands all round again, he departed feeling somewhat blue.

But strange sounds and sights very soon took his attention, and before he was aware of it, he was in the metropolis, surrounded by strangers. Hastening to the Doctor's residence, he found him social and agreeable. Shortly after partaking of dinner with the doctor's family, he went in search of Gnitle's brother. Frank found him very busy, but nevertheless, overjoyed to see him. As Frank was leaving, he gave him his card and number, saying "I haven't said half I wish to, so I shall expect you to room with me to-night, and as much longer as you desire."

Frank thanked him, and returned to the doctor's feeling a great load had been removed, for it was a privilege he did not like to ask, not knowing whether it would be granted freely.

At the time appointed he went around, and soon found himself in a large and cozily furnished room, where they talked and laughed over the past till almost sunrise.

"I wonder whether we will find as much to keep us from sleep to-morrow night"? said Frank.

"O I guess by the end of the month we'll begin to sleep a little," said the brother, jokingly.

I will not dwell upon their happy hours spent together longer, but simply say they remained room-mates while in the city, and the firmest of friends, then and ever after.

And now I hear you ask "How about Grace—did she graduate"? O yes, and with great distinction, not only receiving the scroll, but the gold medal, with the word "Excelsior" engraved on it. So you see she did not miss her aim. Neither will you, if you try; for, my little friends, that is the only way for you to gain distinction in any pursuit, whether it be for knowledge, wealth, power, happiness, or honor. Methinks you still ask "What did Grace do then? Did she sit down and fold her arms in idleness"? O no! She imparted this knowledge to others with patience and ability. The teacher of a large select school was about to resign, so called on Grace—at several of the parents' request—to ascertain if she would undertake the charge.

"Well," answered Grace, "this is quite unexpected, but nothing would please me better if you think I will give general satisfaction."

"I don't think, but I am sure you would," answered Miss Blake.

Before two weeks had passed around, Miss Blake was married, and Grace filling the position, and I need not add, she was greatly loved by scholars and parents as well.

The last day of August who should enter the schoolroom but Mr. Bonbeaw. Grace was so busy she did not hear his tap, so one of the little girls opened the door.

"Ah, hah"! said Mr. Bonbeaw, extending his hand, "there's nothing like business, but when people are so busy a fellow is obliged to knock a dozen times or more, that seems like rushing matters. Well, as it is nearly three o'clock, I suppose you'll soon dismiss, so with your permission I will wait and walk home with you, as I wish to see Miss Gnitle, too. I called at your boarding house, and ascertained where to find you, and other good news was told me while there. I cannot express how delighted I was, words are inadequate,"

It being three o'clock, Grace dismissed them quietly.

while each little girl bowed pleasantly as she left the schoolroom.

"Come," said Mr. Bonbeaw, "hurry and put on your bonnet, for I must leave here this afternoon. I have written Mr. Livingston I will meet him to-morrow without fail."

As they walked toward home, Mr. Bonbeaw again spoke of the good news that had greeted him. "And now, Miss Grace, as you possess all I wished the pearl to represent, suppose I should say that nothing in this world would give me so much satisfaction and joy as to be the husband of the one in which these two pearls are centered."

"And suppose," answered Grace, "I should say that nothing gives me more happiness than to know I am the choice of one who possesses so many virtues."

"I am too happy to say more now, but when I return, we will arrange to have the wedding come off as soon as possible."

They had now reached the house, and found Gnitle awaiting their return.

"Well, my little miss, you haven't caught up with Grace yet ; you'll be obliged to grow several inches yet."

"You'll see when I get my long dresses on, how tall I look," answered Gnitle.

"Well, put them on when I return ; I must be going now, as Sambo and I have a long distance to drive, and will not reach our journey's end before eleven to-night. So good-by both, till I return."

"Come," said Grace, "I have something to tell you. Let us go up to my room. Well, Gnitle, Mr. Bonbeaw has asked me to marry him."

"Well, I'm not surprised at that," answered Gnitle.

"Well, if you are not, I was," replied Grace, "for I never dreamed he had ever thought of me in that light."

"Some people are very blind to such matters; I'm not. Ever since mama was married to Mr. W——— I have kept my eyes open, for that was an 'opener,' I can assure you. I often think how quietly the whole affair was managed. You had better begin to make some preparation, for he will not be able to tarry long, as his mother is not enjoying good health."

"I shall wait until he returns, which will be in a week or two," answered Grace.

Mr. Bonbeaw, being able to arrange matters with Livingston. returned inside of ten days. He called immediately no Grace, and told her he had received her father's and mother's consent, and asked her how long before she would be in readiness.

"How long a time will or can you give me"? asked Grace.

"I promised mother I would return as soon as possible, and perhaps would bring a bride with me. She was delighted when I told her who it was, and gave me this pearl necklace, saying it was one my father gave her to be married in, and she desired you to wear it likewise, that it may celebrate another important event."

"With the greatest of pleasure," answered Grace, examining it closely; then, opening the locket, asked who it contained.

"Father and mother; they were both quite young when taken," answered Mr. Bonbeaw.

"How much you are like him," added Grace.

"Yes, so people tell me," he answered. Then placing an elegant solitaire diamond ring on the forefinger of her left hand, he said—"This is my second present, and you will receive the third when you have set the day. And now I'm going to suggest something. I would like to have all of those little bright faces present when we are married. Yes, and occupying front seats. It would seem like just so many little angels sanctioning our union."

"O that would be delightful to have them all dressed in white and their heads adorned with roses. I shall continue in school till the day before we are married," said Grace, "but will give the parents due notice so they can be on the lookout for some one to fill my place; and in the afternoon I will tell them to be at the church bright as June roses, and not later than nine, as there will be a short entertainment, and for each to dress in white."

"Better tell them to have the dresses in readiness three days beforehand, and speak of the flowers the afternoon before."

"O yes, that would be best; how thoughtful of you."

"I'll order a wagon-load of candies," said Mr. Bonbeaw.

"And I'll have a quantity of cake baked," added Grace. "I'll write to mama; she makes splendid cake, and I'll get Julia's mother to make some, too."

"Yes, and tie up each one into parcels with a blue ribbon and our card attached, then have some one stationed at the door to hand each their parcels as they pass through."

"O that will be splendid; that will make them remember us, if anything will," exclaimed Grace.

"Now everything is arranged except to appoint the day and hour," said Mr. Bonbeaw.

"Suppose we make it the first Wednesday in October, at 10 A. M."

"That suits me exactly, for that will give us ample time to reach the 12 o'clock train," said Mr. Bonbeaw.

When the all-important day arrived, Grace's relatives, friends, and scholars were all present. Grace, attired in a heavy white corded silk, a very long, rich lace veil, and the pearl necklace and a few white roses pinned carelessly at the throat, looked most charming, and soon was the recipient of the third and crowning present which sealed her happy destiny.

After being congratulated, they passed from the church amid sweet faces beaming with smiles.

"O," said Mr. Bonbeaw, as they entered the carriage, "wasn't it delightful to see those bright faces, and won't they be delighted when they receive their parcels"!

Now we will let our imagination follow each little girl home, while Mr. Bonbeaw and his bride are being congratulated and entertained at Julia's, in the most cordial and befitting manner. Each one we hear say—"O, didn't Miss Grace look charming, and wasn't it kind of her and Mr. Bonbeaw to remember us; the other teacher didn't so much as tell us." "Yes," answered their parents, "it was very considerate of Mr. and Mrs. Bonbeaw, and I hope you will preserve their card and keep it as a relic while you live."

While they are eating their candies and preparing their cake to dream over, we'll return to find Mr. and Mrs. Bonbeaw, ready to start on their journey to Paris, there to be received in the most cordial manner by his mother and friends.

CHAPTER X.

THE wedding day was the topic of conversation for weeks, and I may safely add, for months. Mr. Whenford and family were delighted with Grace's selection. Grace had always been their favorite.

Mr. W——— had given her a pressing invitation to come and make her home with his family as soon as she had graduated. Grace preferred teaching, for she had formed a taste for it while assisting her mother. Like Gnitle, she had been accustomed to the school-room ; she felt nowhere else would she be so much at home, till Mr. Bonbeaw came to claim her as his bride, and transfer her to his beautiful home across the sea.

While they are safely crossing, we will visit our little friends, Gnitle and Julia, who had remained room mates, but spent much of their time with Grace, for they found her a great assistance to them in their studies.

"O," said Julia, deploringly, "how we shall miss her when we sit down to study French and Latin."

"We must learn to depend on ourselves ; Grace had no one to instruct her after school hours, and mama always told me when I asked her the meaning of a word, to get the dictionary and see for myself, and if I did not see it, to search till I found it, then I would be sure to remember it"

"Well," answered Julia, "we'll have some difficult lessons to search out and translate before we graduate."

"Yes," answered Gnitle, "I suppose they will rack our brains a little, but of what use are they unless we make use of them"?

"Very true, but I don't wish to end my days in an asylum, after spending so much time and working hard to graduate."

"No fear, Julia, your head is too well balanced."

Thus these young pupils talked till they fell asleep, to dream of weddings, school, and absent friends.

The next day brought a letter for Gnitle from her brother, in which he wrote:

"I promised the day sister was married, to write you immediately. No doubt you are very lonely; not so with me, for with Frank as a room-mate, one can't be blue, and my business takes up the rest of my time. Why, I scarcely find time to read my papers. Nevertheless, I write to mother as often as possible, and you must do the same.

"Frank says he is getting accustomed to strange sounds and sights, but still prefers old and familiar faces, and hopes you will not be in a hurry to break your neck, as he has not advanced very far in surgery yet. He often talks about the good old times you, Del, and he have had together.

"My employers wish me to travel for them next year, and I shall probably continue doing so till I commence business for myself. So hurry and graduate, and when I can afford to take you, we will travel together. Your affectionate BROTHER."

Gnitle read the letter to Julia, saying as she placed it in the envelope, "There seems to be a way opening for me to travel, but I shall not let him pay my expenses when I shall in a few years have money of my own. I would rather teach until then, and have the more to make my journey a long and pleasant one."

"I think that would be best, so long as you are fond of teaching, and do not consider it a hardship."

"How well Frank remembered what I said in fun," added Gnitle, referring again to the letter. "Brother must have lively times with him, he is so jolly—so like his father. O, by the way, that reminds me of my promise. Yes, I said I would write to his mother once every three weeks, so to-morrow I will write again, or she will chide me when I hear from her. Now we must study to make up for lost time, or I fear we shall not graduate as soon as Grace; she had no one to converse with after school, and I think if we talk less we will accomplish more. I'm not going to speak another word," added Gnitle, "so if you ask me a question and I don't answer, don't be offended."

"O," said Julia, "you'll be the first to speak."

Gnitle said not a word, for she foresaw what Julia was aiming at. They studied in silence for more than an hour. Finally Gnitle remarked—"We ought to call on Del."

"So we had," answered Julia; "let's go for a short time; we can study a little later to-night, and thus make up for it."

Then off they went, taking the brother's letter with them.

"O," said Del, "you are just the ones I desire to see, and I was coming to get you to show me how to translate a sentence."

"Ah," said Julia, "we have a difficult time of it ourselves; we haven't Grace to call on now. But sit down, and we will see; perhaps we can manage it together, for three heads ought to be able to handle one sentence."

They soon translated it satisfactorily, and after reading the letter, started for a walk. When they returned, and were about to leave Del at the gate, she looked lonesome, and said—

" How I wish we all could go to the same school; yes, we could see each other often, whereas, now we don't catch a glimpse of each other once a week."

" Well, how can we when we are obliged to study early and late? I expect to study till half-past ten to-night," added Gnitle, "and to-morrow intend writing three letters: one to mama, one to brother, and one to the doctor's wife. That, with my lessons, will be enough for one day; the next day our lessons will be very lengthy—every other day I find them doubled, so, you see, there's no rest for the wicked."

" Better reform then," answered Del, mischievously, as they walked away.

" Del envies the good times we are having together," said Julia as they walked home.

" No, it is not that, but she has always been with me in school, or where she could see me every day, and she feels the change," answered Gnitle. " I don't feel much like study, but I shall be obliged to apply myself closely to lessons in order to be perfect to-morrow, for the teacher said she would review us thoroughly."

" I did not understand her to say she would review," answered Julia.

" Well, you'll find I'm not mistaken, so you had better prepare yourself for a thorough overhauling," said Gnitle, laughingly.

" Dear me, 'tis nothing but prepare one's self all the time," answered Julia, impatiently.

" You'll have to read the Book of Job, if you go on thus," said Gnitle.

" O, Gnitle, you're a great consoler! Once you told me

to take some of Mrs. Winslow's Soothing Syrup, and now you refer me to the Book of Job, and the next time you will order me to take an opium pill."

"Well," said Gnitle, laughing, "if you don't sit down and go to studying, I'll order you out of the room."

"You'd be after me in less than a minute, coaxing me to return."

"There goes the supper-bell—see who'll get there first."

Julia came out ahead, as she had the start of Gnitle.

"Well, well"! exclaimed Julia's mother, "I'm afraid you two romp and talk more than you study."

"Time will tell," answered Julia.

"Yes, and if that should not, examination day will," answered her mother, significantly.

"It will be necessary for them to have two gold medals this time, with the word 'Excelsior' engraved, or neatly set with diamonds or pearls, as we both are aiming high—higher—highest; yes, I have it now, the last," said Gnitle, mischievously.

"Yes, I dare say you'll receive the medal—for mischief, in that degree," answered Julia's mother, smiling; for she considered them a well-matched pair, and liked to see them full of glee, for in her own mind she was fully convinced they were trying their best.

The next afternoon, Gnitle wrote the three letters; and in less than a week received an answer to each. Her mother wrote her that Mr. W——— would be down for them every other Saturday as long as the warm weather lasted.

The doctor's wife wrote:

"I suppose you will pass through here very often this Summer, so I shall expect to see you each time."

Her brother wrote:

"Frank and I will be up to go a-fishing in August, so you, Julia, and Del be ready to accompany us.

"Frank says he'll try not to go down for bait again, but if he should, he'd like to have you all there to fish him out."

Now I have written a short sentence from each of her letters, and now will go on with the review lesson. Well, it was just as Gnitle said; she examined them thoroughly, but neither missed or blundered over a question she chanced to ask them. And how delighted both were. Yes, more than delighted, for they talked of nothing else till their eyes were closed in sleep.

The next morning both were up early, studying with fresh vigor. The victory gained the day previous had renewed their energy, and prepared them for more vigorous exertion. I came near forgetting to tell you that Grace had written her mother, Gnitle, and brother each a long letter. I cannot say what she wrote her mother and brother, but to Gnitle she wrote as follows:

"MY DEAR SISTER:

"I have a lovely home, and hope some day to see you in it. Mr. Bonbeaw wishes me to say, when you arrive at the age of eighteen, he shall expect you to make us a long visit, and dear sister, it may be forever, if you are so disposed. Yours affectionately, GRACE."

This is only a small portion of the letter, for Grace hoped she would persevere with her studies, and likewise charged her not to neglect the Sanctuary.

Mr. Whenford did not forget his promise to come for Gnitle and Julia every other Saturday. Each time, Gnitle called at the doctor's, likewise to see her uncle and aunt, for she was greatly attached to both; they had been so kind to her from the first of her stay till the last.

In August, Gnitle and Julia had their vacation, and so did Del and Nenie. Mr. W——— came for Gnitle and Julia, and Del's brother for her and Nenie. This brother had married Mr. Whenford's daughter, who was next to the youngest. So these young folks were all together again, to tread old and familiar haunts. All they required now to make their happiness complete, was for the brother and Frank to make their appearance among them.

So one fine day the doctor drove down to meet them. When the boat landed, both were there waiting anxiously, lest something in his practice might prevent his coming. But they did not wait long.

The doctor, in his jolly way, said—" Well, my boys, here you are. Jump in, for all the folks are waiting impatiently, and have been imploring me to hurry."

" So all hands are waiting, you say, father " ?

" Yes, if you mean girls."

Sure enough—there they were to meet them as they drove up. Mrs. W———, with the rest, stood at the gate. Such hand-shaking ; well, I'm sure there were some lame wrists in that jolly crowd the next day.

How much these young people enjoyed their vacation, rambling through orchards and groves, rowing up and down stream, riding and fishing, I'll leave for you to picture, for it would be useless for me to make the attempt. But one thing I am quite certain of, that Frank did not forget to call on his " life preserver," as he always called him, this time presenting him with a gold pen.

" Another useful present, my boy," said he. " Why, I wouldn't mind plunging in and saving a dozen lives per week at this rate."

After holding pleasant conversation a short time, they then parted, with a promise from Frank to see him again before returning to the city.

"Well, well," said all whom he had left fishing in the stream just above, "you staid so long we began to think of coming with our hooks."

"No need of that when I had a 'life preserver' so near," answered Frank.

Now came invitations to suppers—first to the doctor's, then to Mrs. W———'s; next to Gnitle's aunt's; finally, to Del's brother's. Thus vacation sped swiftly, and before they were aware of it, all were making preparations to return, each looking the picture of health, and ready to follow their several pursuits.

The young ladies applied themselves with fresh vigor in the pursuit of literary attainment, while the young gentlemen were equally energetic in their respective callings.

Now, while they are all busily engaged, we will return and see what is the matter at Mr. Whenford's, for the doctor has been calling there two and three times a day, so there must be something of a serious nature. Sure enough, such is the case. A deadly type of dysentery had spread through that part of the country, prostrating Mr. W———, Hal, Sir Walter, and Mr. Whenford's mother, then eighty-seven years old, and had never known what severe sickness was till then. Age and declining strength being against her, she only lived a week after being seized with the malady. Next a married son was taken down with it, and lived just one week and died; next a sister, and finally another married son buried two beautiful children in one grave. Meanwhile Mr. W———, Hal, and Sir Walter were lying at the point of death.

Night and day found Mrs. W———, the youngest daughter, and Deaun—who was now a servant in Mr. Whenford's family — at their bedside. Hal was the youngest, and had always been a great pet of his father's. They both occupied a large room during their sickness. Mr. W——— could not be prevailed on to leave it for another, and so heard his every moan, which were many before he died.

Mr. W——— and Sir Walter recovered slowly, never to enjoy good health again. It left Mr. Whenford very nervous, and not being able to sleep, brain fever set in, from which he never recovered.

Sir Walter suffered from weak lungs for several years, and died with consumption.

Mrs. Whenford had kept everything from Gnitle, knowing she could do no good, for everybody avoided coming in contact with it; and not only that, but it would have worried her and taken her mind from her studies. Of course she knew all about Mr. Whenford's last sickness, and attended his funeral, and so did the brother.

Mrs. Whenford remained at the homestead only long enough to have the property sold, and receive her third. She then went back to the house in which her mother died, and where she had brought up her little family in joy and content, feeling they were all she had on earth to live for. But what a precious *all* they were to the mother.

Sir Walter travelled for his health, while the youngest sister went with him as far as Texas, to visit a married sister, and finally married and settled there too.

And now of this once large and healthy family, there are only two or three living.

Deaun went with Mrs. W———, but finally remained with the sister, for Deaun could never be prevailed on to leave the quiet little village. " For," said she, " dis is my home, and eberybody knows me, and I knows eberybody; so here Deaun must stay till de bref goes out ob her body."

Del's parents were very anxious to have her live with them again, but Deaun firmly declined.

The latter part of May, Julia and Gnitle graduated. Gnitle was the only young lady that received an "Excelsior" medal. Gnitle was delighted, and wrote immediately to Grace and her brother, and in a short time received an answer of congratulation from each. Both spoke of their mother being a widow again, and hoped Gnitle would try hard to cheer her declining years.

" Ah," said Gnitle to Julia, "the cheering part all falls on me after all. They all said mama would have some one to cheer her when she married Mr. W———, but I always felt that she was taking a great charge upon herself, and that she would probably outlive Mr. W———, he being ten years her senior. The only thing I now regret is that she has had so much care and anxiety during all that sickness."

" O, Gnitle, you should not be selfish, for if she had not watched over them, it would have fallen on some one else, perhaps less competent."

" That may be, but I shall always feel she should have remained a widow. 'Once a widow,' my motto is, 'remain so.' "

"Well, Gnitle, everybody thinks differently in regard to such matters, and only a few think as you do."

"Well, our school days are over, and soon we shall part for the balance, perhaps, of our lives. If so, we have been happy together, haven't we"? asked Gnitle, kissing her.

"Ah, yes! too happy—and to think it cannot last," said Julia, in tears.

"We can see each other during the Summer, for mama and I will board with aunt till Fall.

In the Autumn, Gnitle and her mother concluded to return with the brother and board in the city. He and Frank having made their usual August visit, all returned together. Del's father again sold out, and came to the city to engage in business. The stepmother, Del. Nenie, and himself boarding in a large and fashionable hotel. Gnitle and her mother, the son and Frank, were boarding in a private family. Frank and Gnitle were not long finding Del and Nenie. As there was not so much studying to be done, they saw each other very often, until Gnitle again became a teacher, "not a little one, but a tall one then."

Gnitle had expressed a wish to teach several times in the presence of the doctor, with whom Frank was studying. Accordingly, one day hearing Mrs. Duval say she would soon require another French and Latin teacher, he spoke favorably of Gnitle, and concluded to give her a note of introduction to Mrs. Duval. She and her daughter being well pleased with Gnitle's appearance, engaged her services from the first of November.

"Then," said Gnitle, "I shall feel happy once more, for I don't like to sit down and fold my arms when I can benefit others and myself as well."

"I often feel, if I was younger, that I would like to teach again," said her mother.

"O mama, you have taught long enough, and have had too much care already, so do try and take the world easy, and when I am eighteen perhaps you and I will pay Grace a visit."

This pleased and cheered the mother, and that was what Gnitle took delight in doing, for Gnitle had made up her mind that she was the one, and the only one designed to cheer her mother's declining years. Whenever she returned from school and found her mother serious or gloomy, she did her utmost to make her forget the past. But how apt we all are to dwell on it, whether it be bright or gloomy.

The year passed around pleasantly, Gnitle giving entire satisfaction. During her vacation all met in the country once more. But this was a sad meeting for all. Gnitle's mother sickened and died suddenly while there, leaving Gnitle and her brother to come back alone, grieving and despondent.

"O," said Gnitle, when she came home from school one day and beheld the large Bible, "if I could only see her poring over these pages once more, what would I not give."

And now while I'm reminded, I'll pen the lines written by Gnitle—the following Summer—while sitting near her mother's grave. The Book from which she had derived consolation was chiseled on the stone. Except the little Gnitle was able to give, she found this her greatest consoler. Hence the lines that inspired Gnitle wrote while seated there :

TO MOTHER.

Mother, thy tombstone I see is tipped;
Is it the fault of the setter?
Or have strong winds in frosty weather
Rudely blown, and icy water dripped
Around thy head?

Once an icy finger did thee touch,
Thy warm, and loving heart did still;
And now, thy crumbling form helps fill
The space reserved, with new-made earth—
Lent, now returned!

An emblem chiseled on thy tomb
Of what in life, thou held most dear,
And always gave thy spirit cheer,
And bade it rise, dispel its gloom
Is opened there!

O blessed reminder! bringing thee back
To me, as in life I still see thee;
Poring o'er its pages hopefully:
Trusting all to Him: in faith no lack;
Blessed Comforter!

Now thy sacred dust, I here must leave!
Thy earthly friend, and guide is nigh;
Dost thou see it from on high?
And does it still bright visions weave
Of coming joys?

My eyes have seen. my ears have heard,
More than its pages ever told !
Now where streets are paved with gold,
And free from earth's alloy, I praise the Lord
Eternally.

The closing verses of this beautiful poem leads one to feel that mother and daughter were in direct intercourse.

The conception, or answer to Gnitle's question seems to indicate that she felt fully assured all was well ! And that even more was in store for the departed, than she had here anticipated.

The quiet solemnity of the spot chosen, too, suggests that Gnitle wished to be near the one there resting in body, as well as in thought.

It again shows how devoutly attached she was to those near and dear to her ; and it is this in her nature that made every one love her, and makes every one she comes in contact with esteem her now.

In the possession of a nature thus genuine, no one need be without friends.

Gnitle's brother being about to leave the city, to be gone at least a year, she concluded it would be better to board with Mrs. Duval.

The more they were together, firmer grew their friendship.

And as this grew, more confidence did Mrs. Duval feel she could repose in Gnitle ; so unbosomed her past freely to her.

Sitting quite alone one day, with Gnitle, she told about

their being shipwrecked, and the hardships they had been obliged to endure.

"Nevertheless," she added, "could my dear husband and son been saved, I could have endured it without a murmur. But to think daughter and I are left to struggle alone." Then she stopped, too full to utter more.

"I am sure you have been very successful," answered Gnitle.

"O yes, but there has been a great deal of care attending it. And I was never accustomed to much of that. I know I have great reason to be thankful, but I wish circumstances could have been ordered differently."

"Yes," said Gnitle, we all feel in that mood sometimes; but if we can only feel—that—Providence wisely has mingled the cup; we soon learn to forget our troubles."

Thus they consoled, and talked over by-gone associations, many times after school hours. Gnitle grew very fond of her daughter, and often asked her if she would like to travel. So one day after Gnitle had passed her eighteenth birthday, she told Mrs. Duval she thought of taking a trip with her brother to Paris, and that she would be delighted if she would allow her daughter to accompany them.

"I should be highly pleased to have her do so, could I afford it."

"O," said Gnitle, "it shall never cost you a penny! If you will only consent to her going, that is all the recompense I shall require."

"I could not think of your paying her expenses. I will pay the cost of going, and hand you the balance when you return."

"Then," said Gnitle, "give her as much as you think she will require for candy, flowers, nicknacks, etc., and let me be responsible for the rest. You may just as well consent first as last to this, for I shall have my own way in the end," laughingly said Gnitle. "For you know had I not really wished her to accompany us, I should not have made the proposition."

"Very well, it shall be as you wish. When do you think of starting"?

"Not before Spring," answered Gnitle.

"The month will depend upon brother. He cannot always leave just when he would like."

"I will be getting her in readiness gradually, so it will not interfere with my school duties. I shall find the greatest difficulty in getting one to fill your place."

"Hope not, I think Miss Shay quite competent, and her mother being a widow, might be pleased to have her teach."

"I was thinking of her. I will speak to her the first opportunity that offers."

In a few days after this conversation, Mrs. Shay called on Mrs. Duval, and during this call the conversation led to teaching.

"I do so wish," said Mrs. Shay, "my daughter could get a position in some school to teach French and Latin."

"There will be a vacancy here in the Spring. If you so desire, you may consider her services engaged," replied Mrs. Duval.

"One more load off my mind," said the widow, gratefully.

"And off mine, too; so we will consider it settled," replied Mrs. Duval in her cheerful and ladylike manner.

Gnitle wrote Grace immediately after her mother's death, and received this answer:

"DEAR SISTER:—It pained me much to hear of mama's death; but, inasmuch, I know, and feel, her spirit still lives with Christ, Our Saviour! for if ever there was a Christian and devoted mother, she was one. And now dear Gnitle, whatever mama has left of worldly goods is yours and brothers; so divide it equally between you.

Mr. Bonbeaw says we have more now than we shall probably need; in a few days he will send you a paper legally drawn, which we will sign in the presence of witnesses. Likewise, have their names attached, so you can proceed to settle affairs immediately. And as soon as all is divided equally and settled between you, I shall then expect a visit from both. Mr. Bonbeaw says you must certainly comply with grandma's request."

"Of course I shall," said Gnitle, "hav'nt I always intended to? and is'nt it kind of them to give up all claim to mama's estate? Well, I shall have plenty to travel with, and keep me, as long as I live, and I mean to do all the good I can with my inheritance, too." I'm not going to dress in lace, and wear diamonds, as some do, and see my neighbors in need. No, not I"! Thus Gnitle soliloquized, after reading the letter. The legal document soon arrived, for which Gnitle wrote a letter of thanks immediately, and finished by saying "you may expect to see us in the Spring."

The property, divided equally with grandma's bequest, and what Gnitle had saved while teaching, enabled her to prepare for the expected journey, feeling perfectly independent and happy. The evening before they were to sail, who should call but Frank, Del, and Nenie, to wish them a prosperous voyage. After passing a delightful evening, each gave her a small keep-sake as they were leaving. Of sad looks and tears, I'll write nothing, only leave you to imagine how sad and lonely Frank, Del, and Nenie were, to be left thus behind after years of true and lasting friendship.

CHAPTER XI.

THE day proved most favorable, and so the weather remained, 'till they were safely in Paris, and seated comfortably in the hotel, in which the brother always felt perfectly at home.

"Now," said Gnitle, "I will surprise Grace by sending her my card."

"Well," said Grace to Bonbeaw, "just think of Gnitle's being at a hotel, and I residing within a stone's throw of her. That's just like brother, so independent."

"Never mind, I'll soon settle that. Sambo and I will drive around for them immediately," answered Bonbeaw. And before they were aware of it, Mr. Bonbeaw was there with the carriage and they all seated in it, and in twenty minutes these dear children were once more together. And what a meeting, after so much had transpired. Happy and sad! Sometimes wreathed in smiles, and a moment later in tears. Like an April day was their first week together. The brother having some important business to transact at Havre, left them, to be gone two months—saying he would then return for them, and then they would proceed to London, Nottingham, Manchester, and thence to Edinburgh, and after remaining there a month, would sail homeward.

"We shall not consent to their making us so short a visit," said Mr. and Mrs. Bonbeaw.

"Ah, but I'm their pilot; they will be obliged to go in whatever direction I may see fit to steer. Better make the most of their time, and visit all the places of interest, as that is quite as long a time as I can possibly give them," said the brother, before departing.

Every day Sambo was driving them to some new scene of interest. Mr. Bonbeaw was determined nothing should escape their notice; "for," he remarked, "I mean this visit to be of use to both. At some future day that young lady—pointing toward Gnitle—can, after paying strict attention to whatever is worthy of note in her travels, make a fortune by using her imaginative mind and pen.

"O, don't flatter me, I'm very susceptible!" answered Gnitle.

Their evenings were generally spent at home. Miss Duval and Grace entertaining them with their sweet and powerful voices. Bonbeaw and Gnitle were always silent and delighted listeners.

. One evening while Grace and Miss Duval were singing, a gentleman called to see Mr. Bonbeaw on business of importance; showing him into the library, which was situated at the farther end of the hall, they proceeded to arrange the matter between them.

"O what a sweet voice!" exclaimed the lawyer. And when she had finished singing "Mary of Argyle," he rose to his feet, saying, "O, how sweet! I would like to see its possessor."

"She is just as charming as the voice," and if you will

come with me, I will give you an introduction to her, and to Miss Gnitle, my wife's sister."

"Not now, but to-morrow evening I will be most happy to come and bring my son, if it will not interfere with your arrangements for the evening."

"We are generally at home evenings, and always pleased to see our friends. So I shall expect to see you."

"I shall not disappoint you, for I would not miss such a musical entertainment for the world," answered the lawyer. Then bidding Bombeaw good-night, departed; the voice still ringing in his ears, and saying to himself, "how much like hers."

When he reached the hotel, which he had always considered home, and probably the only one he would ever dwell in here, he said to his son, "I have made an engagement for you to-morrow evening; will you be at leisure"?

"Yes, father, and I'm delighted to hear you speak of going out, for you need recreation."

"Well, we will hear some sweet singing, and I would travel some distance to hear as good as I listened to last night, while in Mr. Bonbeaw's library.

"Yes, and I would travel some distance to catch a glimpse of those faces again. They were at this hotel, and I saw them when Mr. Bonbeaw drove away with them," answered the son.

"Well, you may look at their faces while I listen to their singing," replied the father.

Punctually they kept the appointment with Mr. Bonbeaw, and he in turn introduced them to the young ladies. They were soon asked to sing. Miss Duval being asked first, took her place at the piano with perfect ease, and sang several pieces in succession, for she was no sooner through with one, before the lawyer and son were selecting another.

Next Mrs. Bonbeaw presided there, while the young ladies sang several accompaniments. When they were through singing, the lawyer and son, finding it was much later than they were aware of, arose to go.

"Hope we shall have the pleasure of meeting you again," said Gnitle.

"Thank you, nothing would afford us more pleasure, and if you remain long, no doubt we shall call frequently."

"Then we shall not have the pleasure of meeting you again during this visit, as we leave to-morrow."

"I am sorry to hear you say so," answered both father and son.

"Don't forget that Mrs. Boubeaw and I shall be pleased to see both any time you choose to favor us with a visit."

"Thank you, we shall accept your invitation, and call perhaps more times than you will appreciate."

"We'll see to that; don't fear," said Mr. Bonbeaw, jokingly.

Then shaking hands with all, and wishing the young ladies a pleasant journey, they departed.

"Did you notice that they addressed me as Miss Duvar"?

"No," answered Mr. Bonbeaw, "I thought I spoke your name plainly; why did you not rectify the mistake"?

"O, I thought it made little difference, as I should probably never meet them again."

When the lawyer and son were walking home they remarked that their names would be the same by changing the last letter to *l*. The next day early in the morning the brother arrived.

"Come," said he, "I'll just give you time to eat break fast, and then we must be off. Business before pleasure, you know, is my motto, for I'm bound to be a rich man."

"Yes, but don't think that is all you have to live for," answered Grace.

"You are right, sister, and I appreciate your reproof."

Then after taking an affectionate leave of each other, proceeded on their journey. Not long after the lawyer and son called on Mr. and Mrs. Bonbeaw.

While asking after the young ladies, Mrs. Bonbeaw noticed that he did not speak the name correctly, so she remarked that it was rather a strange coincidence, their names being the same.

"What! you don't tell me her name is Duval"? and seemingly much agitated, but in a low, subdued, half unconscious tone, said, "Ah! can it be that I've been listening to my own daughter's voice. Can it be! Ah, can it be! Do tell me all you know in relation to her"!

"Well," said Mrs. Bonbeaw, "her mother is a widow and keeps a noted school, in which sister taught French and Latin. A strong attachment was formed, and the mother decided to let the daughter travel with them."

"Have you her address"?

"I have, and will give you one of her cards.'

"When do you think they will return home?"

"Some time in September."

"My son and I will endeavor to reach there when they do, or before, if possible. This news has quite overpowered me. I will go home and take something to quiet my nerves."

"Wait a moment, Sambo and I will drive you there in a hurry."

When they reached the hotel they assisted him to reach his room. After giving him a nerve mixture, they succeeded partially in quieting him for the time being. Nervous prostration lasted several weeks, but loyalty to those he now believed were still alive, roused him to action. He finally made up his mind the time had come to sail, in order that all might reach New York city about the same time.

Not wishing to cause any unnecessary excitement during school hours, he concluded to wait, or defer the visit until evening.

As they ascended the steps, the same sweet voice attracted their attention. Mr. Duval stood like one spellbound. Then said he "I'm too unstrung to pull the bell."

"I'll do it, father," kindly said the son.

The door was opened by a servant and they were ushered in the parlor. Yes, and in the presence of those he had always thought dead until so recently.

"O," exclaimed Mrs. Duval, "is it reality or is it a dream"?

"O my darling wife and daughter," said he, as he held them both in fond embrace. "It is reality of the brightest kind"!

"And who may this be"?

"Your baby boy, now a man."

The last scene was too much for Gnitle, and with tears streaming from her eyes, she sought her room. Then kneeling down, thanked her Heavenly Father that she had been instrumental in thus bringing this loving family together.

And now let me surprise you; just one year from that day Gnitle became the wife of Mr. Duval's son, and took her second trip to Paris, and is now the mother of five beautiful children.

Now I suppose you will wish to know all about Frank, Del, Nenie, and the brother.

Frank married Nenie, and now lives in Chicago, and is the father of two lovely children. He likewise became a skillful surgeon and physician.

Del never married, but not for lack of offers, I can assure you.

Gnitle's brother married Mrs. Duval's daughter, and is now a wealthy and retired merchant, and is the father of two sons and a daughter.

Mr. Bonbeaw and wife are still living in Paris, and have four bright children. Mrs. Bonbeaw died shortly after her son's marriage.

Del's father died, and the step-mother married again, and is still living near Gnitle's aunt and uncle, who are now quite old, but enjoying very good health. Poor old Deaun lived with them 'till she died, and was buried near the quiet little village.

The doctor and wife are still a jolly and happy couple, and every Summer expect a visit from Frank and his family, Gnitle and Del.

Gnitle's brother frequently joins them, and there is a jolly time all round.

All the old familiar haunts are visited, and you know, or will in a few years realize, how delightful it is to roam where your little feet have strayed during your school days. Ah, yes, it will afford you great happiness to visit the home of your youth—the garden, the swing, the orchard, the pond, the spring, and the "Old Oaken Bucket," as well.

"Surprises come in various forms, and I have just had a very pleasant one."

"In what shape do you think it came"?

"Why, in the form of Gnitle herself. Just as I had finished my story, who should the servant usher in the parlor but Gnitle. I knew her voice immediately, and without a moment's delay, hastened to invite her to my cosy sanctum."

"O," said she, seating herself by my pleasant grate fire," "this seems like old times."

"Yes," I answered, "but there are no andirons and back-log. Inasmuch, this is very cheerful, so we won't complain," she replied.

Then turning quickly around, and seeing such a pile of manuscript on my table, asked what it meant.

"O," I answered, "it is a story for young misses I've just completed. I had just wiped my pen, to lay it away as you entered the parlor."

"There is nothing I enjoy more than reading a story especially prepared for the young. Will you not just read to me a part now, and let me come to-morrow to hear the ending"?

"Certainly, it will afford me much pleasure."

So we sat down again near the pleasant fire, and I commenced reading, and when I had finished part of my story, she exclaimed "O how truthful"! And when I came to "first impressions being lasting," "O, that," said she "reminds me of something I have never told you; so stop reading for the present, and I will tell you how I impressed a would-be murderer: "One night, just before this—my third trip to Paris—my husband had occasion to be away from home over night, and I was left alone in the house with the servants. I never was the least timid, so thought nothing about it. In the middle of the night I awoke suddenly, and beheld a man standing over me with something in his hand. With great presence of mind, I said 'take anything you like, but spare me to my children,' two of whom were sleeping beside me. He slipped whatever he had in his pocket, pointed toward heaven, kissed his hand to me, and disappeared. From his movements I knew I was perfectly free from harm, but still the shock had rendered me too nervous to sleep."

"The next day, when I told my husband, he said I must have been dreaming."

"Yes," said I, "with both eyes open."

He then examined the door and windows, and still came to the conclusion I was dreaming, but I firmly said my eyes were open.

So shortly after I returned from Paris, I received an envelope bearing the postmark California. Opening it, I found a note which read as follows:

"DEAR LADY:—You saved me from a wretched life, and a miserable end. I shall die blessing you and yours."

Then affixed was a ☞, ——, ●

I suppose the hand (pointing upward) meant I had reminded him of his mother in heaven, or some dear friend; the dash was to serve for the name he would rather conceal than divulge (don't blame him); and the blot a kiss or a tear of contrition.

"Well," said I, "I suppose your husband's doubts are all removed"?

"O yes," she answered, smiling.

And then I said "if you have no objection, I will note down what you have just told me."

"Certainly, none whatever, and when I call to-morrow I will bring a poem, or several, from which you can select such as you think will best carry out your purpose, for I perceive your story has a mission, and as you have chosen me for it's heroine, an honor for which I am truly grateful I shall consider it a favor to assist you in what you assure me has been a pleasant pastime."

And now as she has listened to the remainder of my story, and sanctions my effort thus far, I will endeavor to choose such of her poems as I have reason to believe would have been her selection, for reasons expressed fully in the above paragraph, and add them to my surprise, hoping the part added may serve to make the book still more interesting, and I trust, ennobling.

But I fear I shall not be able to select as many as I should like, on account of the length of those selected.

Nevertheless, when I tell you why I have chosen these, I feel you will be fully satisfied and appreciative.

"Water It Shall Be," explains itself.

"Me Too," it seems some friend of Gnitle's met the strawberry woman and little girl, so told Gnitle about them. Hence the poem "Me Too," written in the middle of the night, as she feared totrust her memory until morning.

"*WATER IT SHALL BE.*"

Once I had a mother kind,
  Who loved her children three,
And felt no sacrifice too great
  For these so full of glee.

Reared in plenty, though not in wealth,
  Queenly was her bearing,
E'en from her childhood, I've been told,
  Few equalled her in learning.

No matter what the case might be,
  If a word she chanced to see—
Whose meaning was not clear to her,
  Down came Webster instantly.

In grammar and arithmetic
  Few could with her compare,
When many tried to puzzle her,
  She proved her gifts were rare.

When young a state certificate
  Was meted unto her ;
This she prized, but did not feel,
  'Twould prove a mine to her.

She married in a family rich,
  In slaves, as well as gold,
Their table decked with utmost care
  Of wine and brandy told.

Yes, luxury seemed spread out there,
  Each child a portion had,
To go and spend as they thought best,
  To cheer or make them sad.

My parents sought their fortune West,
And so it might have proved,
Had not typhoid's fevered hand
Seized her my father loved.

Very sick was she for weeks and months,
Strangers were very kind ;
Restored to health, she then returned
To grandma, "good and kind."

But 'twas to learn the sad, sad news,
"Grandpa had lost his gold"!
Politics and speculation wild
Many acres now had sold.

Grandma's too, was nearly gone
By signing o'er her wealth,
A house, a lot, and woodland wild,
A ninety-dollar pension left.

Grandpa had been a soldier bold,
For liberty he fought,
So his memory I'll cherish ever,
E'en hazardness my portion bought.

Grandpa was called to his long home
After a year of helplessness ;
Palsy had shook his manly form,
And robbed his spirit's cheerfulness.

Grandma lived to a good old age,
And ne'er was heard complain,
She had a Christian's cheerful heart,
Which eases every pain.

Her children reared in affluence,
'Twas hard to lose their wealth,
Some sought a refuge in the cup,
And thus they ruined health.

For pa, who ne'r had thought of work,
'Twas very hard indeed,
For now a wife, and children three,
He had to clothe and feed.

He then indulged in brandy red,
Which made his temper rise;
"Now Charles," said ma, "I can't endure,"
Tears glist'ning in her eyes.

"Three children God has given you,
They're bright and pretty, too,
So do for sake of them and me,
The fatal cup eschew."

"I know that all you've said is true,
That you have talents, too;
That you have led a Christian life,
Which can be said of few."

"But still you know what habit is,
I've used it since a boy,
But still I'll try to give it up,
Since you it does annoy."

But still she felt the tempter's reign,
So sought her mother's roof;
Her darling boy she left behind,
With pa and grandma as proof—

She felt and knew he would receive
The very best of care.
How many, many there are here
Who have no roof to share.

She had a mother's roof, and mine
I told you of at first;
A mine that proved fine gold to her,
And placed us with the first.

And now 'tis more than gold to me,
To hear, as oft I have,
She who with patience taught me most,
Lies silent in the grave.

I too, shall always cherish him
"Who said shall water be,"
And never, never broke his word,
Spoken thus mournfully.

He came one night, and on his knee
He placed my tiny form,
Then gently pressed my little head,
And drew it near his own.

His look was sad, ah, very sad!
He bade his last good-bye,
We little thought when pledged his word
By water he would die.

Not feeling well, he thought a sail
Would buoy his spirit up,
So with a friend he hastened down
And took his seat upon the dock.

Said R——, "now Charles, you look unwell,
Do swallow some for me."
"O no! I've said shall water be,
So thus shall ever be."

His friend went back for hook and line,
To fish while sailing o'er,
When he returned my father rose,
And sank to rise no more.

The doctor said a faintness came,
And then a spasm ensued,
Which took away his power to swim,
And then king death pursued.

He left us one sure pledge indeed,
He loved his children three,
When he refused the fatal cup,
"Water it Shall Be."

Hoping that you will inscribe on your heart's banner the motto—"Water it Shall Be," I will now proceed with "Me Too," and then add the word—FINIS.

ME TOO.

While a sunburnt mother
Was crying strawberries—
Bright red, sweet, and fresher
Than sailed o'er the ferries—
Her wee, brown-eyed daughter,
Trudging close beside her,
Holding high her pretty head,
Sprightly and sweetly said—
Me Too!

Me too, with sparkling eyes
  And lips red as cherries,
Went forth with the sunrise
  To pick sweet strawberries
Our breakfast to supply ;
While she went forth to cry,
With heart so young and joyous,
Her sweet bewitching chorus—
      Me Too.

Me too, was all she said,
  Me too, the potent charm,
Turned many a lady's head ;
  And thus her little arm
Unburdened, reached for more,
While the mother did them pour
From her own ; thus relieved,
Felt the magic, and believed
      'Twas in Me Too

What brings this luck to me?
  I heard the mother say,
I surely think I see
  Why I'm in luck to-day!
"'Tis strawberries" I've cried
E'er since her father died ;
But no such luck as this,
'Tis unexpected bliss,
Then low she stooped to kiss
      Me Too.

O what a happy smile
  Passed o'er that lovely face,
While they to rest awhile
  Sat down both face to face;
A lady passing by
Had heard the little cry,
So asked the mother why
She taught the child to cry—
      Me Too.

"Me teach the child, ah, no"!
  'Tis God inspires her thus;
Wee thing, she seems to know
  Her words bring gold to us;
My fairy, all the day,
"A magic wand" I say
Me too, has proved to-day:
Then low she bent to say—
      God bless Me Too!

And since that lucky day
  No other name she knew,
Such blessings on her way
  Are given here to few;
Strawberries go and come,
While in a lovely home
Me too "ice cream" doth eat
With strawberries "so sweet,"
While "wee thing" at her feet
      Lisps—Me Too!

The sunburnt mother too
  Has found a lovely home,
Where just a chosen few
  In shining robes do come;
Their voices sweet and clear—
Harmonious to the ear—
Sound His praise unceasing;
"With such," His praise repeating,
While watching and waiting
        For—Me Too.

FINIS.

www.ingramcontent.com/pod-product-compliance
Lightning Source LLC
Chambersburg PA
CBHW030903050726
47500CB00009B/1004
9783744746359